French Twist

An Amelia Feelgood Mystery

Author's Note

This is a work of fiction. Names, characters, businesses, places, events and incidents are either the products of the author's imagination or used in a fictitious manner. Any resemblance to actual persons or animals, living or dead, or actual events is purely coincidental.

Vivaeris, LLC
www.vivaeris.com
French Twist
©2020 Juliet Chase

Beth McElla
French Twist, an Amelia Feelgood Mystery
ISBN: 978-1-939361-08-0

Reading brought us together - I'm so glad you're here!

-Beth

Chapter 1

❧

At the front of the small ferry, Amelia Feelgood stood three back and tried to steady herself enough not to fall into the darkly tattooed arms of the very large man next to her. A light salty breeze teased at her lungs, tempting her to breathe deep, but she didn't feel stable enough on her feet to take advantage. She'd known heels might cause a few difficulties, but she'd had no idea there wouldn't be a civilized walkway from the ferry's upper deck like there was in Seattle. Nobody had warned her that she'd be balancing on the metal car deck between someone's enforcer and a very shiny motorcycle whose owner was glaring at her as if she was deliberately rubbing her silver coat buckles against his paint job. It wasn't her fault there weren't any railings where they expected people to stand before disembarking. The large tattooed man seemed oblivious to her predicament, his eyes fixed on the shore and his large arms folded across his black leather vest.

The pink suede high-heeled boots had seemed like a good idea when she'd gotten dressed that morning, as they were the only shoes that went with this particular coat, plus they were boots. Everyone knows you need boots in the country. And besides, she liked the way they made her feel tall and in charge. She eyed the several layers of potholes on the gangway and the rapidly closing gap of pale green foaming water between the boat and the dock. Healthy-looking seagulls were waiting on top of the pylons as if hoping to steal away a hapless tourist, or at least some chips. One on the left started calling, which set off a raucous chorus, inciting a few of them to take to the skies. They rode the wind turbulence generated by the ferry like kids on a ride at an amusement park.

Amelia couldn't help but wonder if she should just stay on the ferry and go back. She hadn't packed for the wilderness after all. She was here for a society wedding; the invitation had made it clear that formal wear was expected. It had said nothing about what to wear on the ferry. It was raining lightly, not particularly unusual for a weekend in May, but it could have held off for a few days, in her opinion.

With a final jostle that had her balancing precariously on one foot, the boat docked and ropes were secured. When the deckhands undid the safety net, which didn't look like it would keep even a mild-mannered bicycle from falling off, she found herself carried with the crowd eager to get to their island destination. People started chattering with excitement as though the doors had just opened on a Black Friday sale. Her tattooed neighbor brushed past her and into the waiting arms of a young woman with a fresh face and a battered violin case. As the car engines roared to life behind her, Amelia scurried to stay upright, nearly skipping on her toes to avoid twisting an ankle. Her weekend roller case must have helped give her ballast because somehow she washed up on a normal-looking sidewalk next to the small terminal as the crowd almost instantly dissipated.

She looked around to get her bearings and reached into her over-sized pink tote that was slung over one shoulder. She'd written the name of the hotel on the back of…something. There it was, on the margins of her electric bill that she still hadn't paid. Ravenswood Inn. That had a lovely Jane Eyre-ish ring to it. Maybe it would turn out to be haunted. On second thought, she'd rather it wasn't. This trip might not have been her idea, but there was no reason to waste a long weekend in the country with insomnia. Perhaps there would be a rugged Heathcliff that she could sigh over without actually getting involved. She was willing to be distracted for a weekend, but no more than that.

Amelia was a rather plain woman of average height and build in her mid-thirties (she claimed thirty-two) but with a great deal of flair. This is what she'd been told by her ballet teacher at the age of eight when she'd been laughed out of the recital rehearsal by the other, more graceful girls. Madame Elise, who had once graced the stages of Paris during the war and was tall and elegantly slim, had taken her aside and whispered 'Don't worry about them, ma petite, you have something they will never have. You have flair.' Madame Elise was the epitome of style in young Amelia's opinion. Her silver hair was always scraped back, leaving her dark eyes to dominate an architectural face. Despite age, every move and gesture she made was graceful, even if it was shaking hands with proud mothers in a small Oregon town. Ever since, Amelia had practiced 'having flair' and dreamed of immigrating to the French countryside. She had not met any other citizens of La Belle France since her brief time with Madame Elise, but her heart held confidence that France was where she was meant to be. A nation that revered strong-minded women and strong jawlines. A place where her strengths, and not her looks, would be recognized and celebrated. A place where style still had meaning.

There was always something that got in the way of her going, though. At the moment, it was her silly job for Lyle Communications. She was only six months away from being fully vested in her pension and then, finally, she would look seriously into making her dream come true.

A man shouting, "Anyone for Ravenswood Inn? Anyone here for Ravenswood?" interrupted her thoughts. She rolled her suitcase in his direction, the loud noise of the small wheels on asphalt drowning everything else out. "I am! Are you the shuttle service?"

"Umm, hi. Not exactly. The cart here is for your bags. That's the shuttle part so you don't have to haul them up the steps." He pointed to the hill behind the ferry dock where a set of steep stairs had been cut into the cliff. "By the way, I'm Ralph."

"Hi." Amelia was reluctant to give her name to strangers. They so often started using it in a too-familiar manner. She didn't want or need to know the name of restaurant serving staff either. It created a sense of obligation that she didn't have time for.

Ralph took it in good humor. "I'll give it a few more minutes and then head up with your bags if you like."

"Are you waiting for more than me?"

He shrugged. "Don't know. I meet the passenger ferry every day and the car ferry when it comes once a week. Whoever comes over is who I'm here for." He paused for a second. "You might want to cover your ears. I need to shout again."

Amelia quickly clapped her square hands over her ears, but they weren't quite enough to drown out, "Ravenswood! Last call!" Ralph's voice swooped up and down like an overly enthusiastic train conductor. He clearly enjoyed his job. "OK, looks like you're it. Do you want to take the steps and meet me at the top or come with me up the road?"

"I'll come with you." Amelia sighed with relief. Her shoes weren't up to hiking. The online brochure had made this little island sound so civilized.

"Suit yourself," Ralph responded cheerfully, wheeling his luggage cart around and setting off at a brisk pace up the road. Amelia skittered to keep up. Ralph looked to be about sixty and was surprisingly nimble for his age. Maybe it was all the salt air. They passed long lines of parked cars queued to get on the ferry as it continued its inter-island loop. Amelia eyed them with interest. What brought non-wedding guests to the island or prompted the locals to leave it?

"So, what brings you to Findlater Island?" Ralph inquired politely.

"Oh, my um, boss is getting married this weekend. The Lyle-Hammond wedding?" It was still hard for her to think of smarmy Tony Lyle as her boss. His father had been the owner of Lyle

Communications until his untimely death four months ago. She still wasn't clear on exactly how he had died. He had seemed fit and healthy the last time she'd seen him at work. Every time she asked Tony about it, he brushed it off as 'family business' and told her to wear something sexier to the office in the future.

"Ah, yes." Ralph interrupted her thoughts. "Lots of rhinestones."

"Is it?" That sounded awfully ghastly or maybe it was ghastly awful.

"He must be a pretty good boss for you to come to his wedding." Ralph didn't even try to hide his prying.

"You would think that, wouldn't you?" Amelia was no stranger to deflection. Tony was a horrible boss and the only reason she was here was because he'd said he'd fire her if she wasn't; he'd even gone so far as to dig out her job description where it said 'other duties as assigned'. She wasn't so sure Labor & Industries would interpret it the same way, but it would also take them more than six months to even look at a complaint. At which point she intended to be living in France, finally learning how to relax.

"Here we are," Ralph announced cheerfully, bringing his cart to a stop in front of a gray-shingled mansion with two turrets at the front corners. Five or six seagulls were perched in a line on the roof ridge, staring out to sea. A glass-paned door had been painted green to match the climbing vine that hung over it, partially obscuring the red neon 'Welcome' sign. Ralph unloaded her case from the cart, opened the door and carried it in. "Morning Becky! Here's a new guest for the wedding!"

"Coming!" came a voice from the back room.

Amelia glanced around the small lobby. It must have been the original foyer of the house. An all-weather carpet in shades of blue and green had been installed and a small oak hotel desk placed on the long wall. A single oil painting of a storm at sea adorned the wall behind the desk and there were two open arched doors on either end. No other furnishings or creature comforts were to be found. Becky came in carrying a tall vase of pink flowers. Amelia recognized the roses in the mix but that was the extent of her knowledge. She'd never been a gardener. The young woman of about twenty-five had a fresh round face adorned with a spray of freckles. Her light brown hair was scraped back tight in a ponytail and her blue uniform was about five sizes too big. She set the vase down on the end of the desk and smiled at Amelia. "Good morning! How was your trip over? I'll be happy to get you checked in." She did as promised and after Amelia had handed over her credit card, sighing at having to use her personal card for a so-called business expense, Becky handed her a computerized room key. "Room 217. It's right through there," she pointed at the left arch "down the hall and up the stairs. Then it's about midway on the left."

Amelia looked around for Ralph to carry her bags up, but he had disappeared. So with a grimace, she put the room key in her pocket and hoisted her tote bag over her shoulder while extending the handle on her small suitcase. She straightened her spine and flipped her hair back. She intentionally offset her square jaw with a swinging bob of jet-black hair reminiscent of the 1920s. It was straighter and blacker than it would be without the amazing and expensive skills of her hairdresser, Catrine, but she figured part of having flair was knowing who to turn to and what to prioritize.

When Amelia reached the midpoint in the upstairs hallway and located her room, she paused. The upstairs was quietly elegant with a rose-colored wallpaper and brass sconces scattered down the hall. The dark oak floors were covered with a floral carpet runner in dark green. She inserted the plastic card in the door slot. Amazingly, it not only worked on the first try, but the door automatically opened. She was so used to hotel locks turning off, if they worked at all, before she could get to the handle that she'd already started shifting her bag to make a grab for it. The open door threw her balance off and she found herself tripping headfirst into the room with an oomph as her forward momentum was eventually stopped by the bed.

It was nicely made up. Crisp white linens rested under a blue and white striped coverlet. Heavy navy curtains helped the nautical theme along. The walls were whitewashed oak paneling and the furniture was all refurnished antiques or at least vintage rather than the usual high-gloss dark wood hotel chains seemed to favor. There was a slightly woodsy citrus scent in the air as though someone had given it a splash of expensive room spray after cleaning. Maybe this was going to be a good weekend after all. She didn't have to stay at the wedding reception once dinner was over, right? Nobody was going to notice if she wasn't dancing, and she didn't dance anyway. Not that much had changed since her days of ballet class.

Amelia walked over to the heavy drapes and pulled them back with the use of the long clear plastic wands attached to the top. They revealed a stunning view of the sea with just a narrow edge of the cliff directly below the window. She took a step back. The floor-to-ceiling window didn't open and it looked sturdy enough, but Amelia wasn't prepared to take any chances. The automated warning from the city subway played in her head, 'please do not lean on the doors'. It only made sense to apply that to windows overhanging cliffs as well. She stood there and soaked in the view for a few minutes. The waves were starting to get small white caps on them, the wind seemed to be picking up a little as the tops of the evergreen trees were also starting to sway. Not enough to be alarming, but perhaps changing her footwear was in order before she started looking for someplace to get lunch.

Tugging her carry-on case up onto the bed, Amelia grimaced at the thought of spending the weekend in her running shoes, which were the only other footwear she'd brought besides her evening shoes for the wedding. She'd only tucked them in because she'd thought there might be a gym. One of the many suggestions her doctor was always giving her for how to relax and lower her blood pressure was to try a little more exercise. Their plain, white newness mocked her from the edge of the case where she'd squished them in. She hadn't even done up the laces yet. She sat down on the bed and bent over to take her boots off. Frowning with concentration, she laced up the sneakers and put them on. They felt okay, she guessed. She stood and bounced in place slightly. Wandering into the bathroom, she stopped and gaped in shock. Somehow, she'd been expecting something beige. But instead, she was met with a glittering wall of tiny gold glass tiles. They twinkled from the walls of the shower and the ceiling overhead. Only the simple mirror over the vanity was unadorned. It was magnificent. She turned around and went back to her tote bag to find her cell phone. She was going to replicate this in her house in France just as soon as she got one. She took a quick picture from the doorway, not even caring that the mirror caught her reflection as she did so.

Amelia figured she might as well unpack before she went exploring since half her bag was on the bed from retrieving the shoes. She carefully hung her vintage beaded dress in the armoire. It was a sea green flapper dress with fabric 'leaves' suspended from the dropped waist. Each one was outlined in little tiny silver sequins. She wouldn't normally have wasted it on a slimeball like Tony, but it was the only truly formal dress she owned and spending money on something new seemed like even more of a sin. She was saving every penny she could for her escape to France, not including Catrine of course. She would need good hair for her French debut more than ever. She'd brought only two other outfits, so putting everything away didn't take very long. She stowed her case at the bottom of the armoire and then slid the room key into her wallet. Time to explore and find some lunch. But just as she reached for her pink coat hanging from a hook in the small foyer, there was a knock on the door.

Chapter 2

❧

Becky from the front desk stood holding a giant gift basket. Even though she'd just checked in ten minutes ago, Amelia only remembered that her name was Becky because it was written on the shiny brass nameplate pinned to her navy blue and white striped blouse. Becky smiled, her ponytail bobbing as she extended the large fruit basket covered in cellophane. "Ms. Feelgood? We meant to have this in your room when you arrived. Please accept it as our welcome to Ravenswood."

"Um, okay." She went to take the basket from her but Becky was already coming into the room so Amelia stood aside as Becky placed it in the center of the small round table by the window. The basket was so large it took up almost the entire surface. Curly blue ribbon fastened the festoon of plastic at the top. Amelia could see a few oranges and a couple of green bananas, but the rest of the contents remained a mystery.

"And ma'am?" Becky continued earnestly, "anytime you would like a complete tour of the hotel, please just let me know. I or Ralph will be happy to show you around and introduce you to your staff."

What a strange turn of phrase. This was really taking hospitality to an all new and not entirely comfortable level. "Oh, I can't imagine that will be necessary. I'm just here for the wedding tomorrow. I'll be leaving on the foot ferry on Sunday."

"Of course, ma'am. Yes, ma'am. Oh! That reminds me." Becky smoothed the navy skirt of her uniform with nervous hands. "Mr.

Lyle left you a message." She closed her eyes as if trying to remember more carefully. "Please come to his room at two this afternoon."

"Ha! Did he say what for?"

"No, ma'am."

"Did he try to grab your rear when he gave you the message?"

Pink rose across Becky's freckled cheeks. "He left the message with Felicity, ma'am. One of the maids that helps out at the desk on my breaks. But yes, Mr. Lyle has um, a reputation."

"Exactly." Amelia grimaced thinking of the last time she'd wrenched her back, sidestepping away from his grabby fat fingers. "So, you'll understand that there's no way in hell that I'm meeting him in his room. Or mine."

"Ma'am?"

"There wasn't any furniture in the lobby that I saw. Are there any conference rooms or public spaces with chairs we could use?"

"Well, there's the library. It's on the other side of reception. There's a table and a couple of chairs in there. Nobody really uses it, just a few guests who grab a book for when they can't sleep or something."

"That will do. Tell Mr. Lyle I'll see him in the library at two."

"Of course, ma'am." Becky turned to leave with just the slightest twinkle in her eye. Amelia thought if Becky were smart, she'd take a poker with her when she relayed the message to Tony. He was such a moron.

Amelia looked back at the fruit basket with curiosity. There could be cookies in there. But then again, she now only had about an hour and a half before she had to meet with the idiot. Other than trying to feel her up again, what could be so important he needed to see her the day before his wedding? Shouldn't he be sweet-talking his bride so she wouldn't run away?

Amelia hadn't actually met her yet, but she kind of assumed Tony Lyle would make any woman's skin crawl. So maybe this one was a lot tougher than the delicate blonde woman Tony had portrayed so prominently in a silver frame on his desk for the last three months.

Until the wedding invitation had come along with the command attendance, she had assumed that the picture had come with the frame, sort of an instant imaginary girlfriend. Making her decision, Amelia grabbed her jacket and went out into the hallway. As she walked to the stairs, a large man with almost no neck and a thick shock of dark hair on his head, in jeans and a khaki jacket, pushed past her and made his way down the hallway towards her room. "Rude," Amelia said under her breath, but loudly enough for him to hear, which was her intention. The man didn't turn around, just continued at a fast pace to the end of the hall where he turned left.

Amelia straightened her jacket and checked that her purse was still zippered shut (it was) and headed down the staircase, wondering how to say 'fruit basket' in French. She'd begun studying the language via an app on her phone three months ago and had made good progress. She could say "Do you live together?" (Vous habitez ensemble?) which seemed a very forward way of starting a conversation and "Do you like fruit?" (Vous aimez les fruits?) but nothing had yet been taught about baskets.

She exited the hotel and started walking down the street in the opposite direction from where she'd come from the ferry. The little map on the back of the brochure she'd picked up at the front desk said there was shopping and a few cafes in this direction and labeled it the 'historic district'. But the map had clearly not been drawn to scale. She walked down the sidewalk until it stopped and became a dirt trail. Wild blackberry vines were scrambling down the hillside and reaching out for her. In full bloom, they were also buzzing with bees. Glancing down at her new white shoes, she saw that the mud had already begun to penetrate. Some of the romance had leaked out of exploring a new place, but she was hungry and knew better than to deal with Tony when her temper was frayed.

By the time she found the edge of the shopping district, her new shoes were beginning to rub a blister on her big toe and her heels. She only kept going because there was no possible way she could have taken a wrong turn. There had been no cross streets or intersections at all. Not even a car had passed her so far. Finally, she saw a little cluster of buildings up ahead. She passed a quaint little antique shop with some old tin buckets filled with red geraniums set out on the steps and then an upscale wine shop that looked completely empty. Finally, a little cafe, 'Vegi Heaven' was next in the row. It was situated in a small medieval-looking building of dark timbers and bright white plaster. It looked very out of place in the Pacific Northwest. Odds were good she wasn't going to get an actual hamburger either, but maybe the fries, which was what she really wanted anyway, were still an option. Her tired feet made the deciding vote and she went in and stood in front of the giant chalkboard that filled one wall to study her options. There was an earthy, mushroomy scent in the air.

It was a scarily healthy menu. Lentils seemed to be the primary ingredient in almost everything. Amelia hated lentils. Looking around, she saw a few of the tables were occupied, mostly by people wearing old hand-knit sweaters and printed crinkly cotton, layered over thermal underwear. The sort of clothes that people who eat lentils religiously would wear. Some kind of mandolin folk music was playing softly over the sound system. She looked over at the smaller chalkboard on the adjacent wall that featured the daily specials. A veggie burger on a sprouted grain roll with root vegetable chips was as close as she was going to get to the cholesterol-laden meal she really wanted. It would have to do. She went up to the patient young man with a blond man bun and scraggly beard waiting by the cash register and gave her order.

"It'll be about five minutes. Have a seat, wherever you like and I'll bring it out to you."

"Thanks."

Amelia supposed he probably wasn't the one to blame for all the lentils, but he was skinny enough to suggest he ate a lot of them. She was only here until Sunday, she reminded herself. She didn't need to make over the town for just one weekend. She picked a small table by the front window and made herself comfortable. She got out her phone to check her messages (she didn't have any) and briefly considered doing her French lesson, but a few of the other patrons were already looking at her strangely so maybe she'd better leave that until she was back in her room. Her lunch appeared before she could consider her other entertainment options, so she put the phone back in her bag and ate. It was surprisingly good. There might have been a few lentils tucked into the veggie burger, but they were sufficiently disguised by the spicy homemade pickles that she decided to let it go. The veggie chips weren't on par with the humble potato variety, but they were crunchy and fairly tasty and the ketchup added some tang.

While she ate, she considered the view out the window. The buildings were an odd hodgepodge of styles. One was honey-colored stone, it was next to a thatched cottage with a sign out front advertising yarn and knitting patterns. Another half-timbered medieval-looking thing sat further along the road.

She dug her phone out again to check the time and realized she'd need to head back soon since her blisters would keep her from moving at normal speed. Darn shoes. She ate two more chips and then went to pay her bill.

She took her time on the way back and tried to walk as flat-footed as possible to avoid rubbing the backs of her heels any more than necessary. She'd have to investigate the oddness of the village area another time and preferably without having to walk to it again. There hadn't been any other restaurants there that she could see and no real ice cream in the offing either. Vegi Heaven had offered six flavors of soy milk pretending to be ice cream but only someone that could still taste lentils in their mouth would want it.

Amelia was seriously starting to hurt as she finally came up to the circular drive in front of the inn. She couldn't wait to get to her room and find something else to wear, even if it meant her evening shoes that didn't have straps across the back. Or maybe she'd just go barefoot.

All thoughts of the pain went out of her head however when she finally entered the lobby to the sounds of multiple women crying. The entrance itself was completely empty. She followed the loud wailing to a small room at the back lined with books, mostly old Readers' Digest condensed editions and well-worn paperbacks. This must be the library where she was to meet Tony. But the two wingback chairs covered in faded rose-colored upholstery were both occupied. One with a stunned young woman of about seventeen in the same blue uniform Becky had been wearing. Tears were rolling down her round cheeks while she gulped for air. The other chair was taken up by a well-conditioned woman of about thirty with a blonde updo wearing a hot pink tracksuit. Most of the noise was coming out of her mouth but her face wasn't moving. It didn't have a line or a crease on it. Her mascara wasn't even running. Too much Botox was Amelia's guess.

"Why would someone do this to me?"

"Do what?" Amelia inquired, intensely curious.

"Kill him, of course. What else would I mean?" The woman finally turned to look at Amelia. "You! This is all your fault."

"It is?"

"Yes!"

Chapter 3

❦

"Err. Let's start again, shall we?"

The blonde and pink woman just kept crying without moving her face. A cloud of strong perfume surrounded her and every now and then it wafted towards Amelia, making her eyes burn. She took a couple of steps back to try to get out of range.

"You seem to know who I am. But I can't say the same. Who are you and who's dead?"

That shut the woman up fast. Now she just gaped in shock. "You don't know who I am? After you tried to break up my engagement?"

"I did?" Amelia was starting to feel the threat of a very circular conversation so she took things in a different direction. "What's your name?"

The blonde woman glared at her with all the fury that a china doll was capable of expressing. It occurred to Amelia that was exactly what this woman resembled, a rather plump china doll with smooth porcelain skin and a face that never moved.

"I'm Heather, Heather Hammond," the woman spit out. "You know, the bride." She added the sarcastic twist at the end before bursting into tears again.

"Oh! Heather, I certainly didn't recognize you from your picture." Heather's only response was to glare even harder. Trying to picture a china doll squinting made Amelia's head hurt. Then it dawned on her. "You don't mean Tony...?"

"Yes. And it's all your fault."

"Tony is dead? And it happened… here?" Tony was a bully and an idiot but she'd never wished him dead. "Did he have a heart attack?"

The other young woman who had just been sitting there leaking now started actively crying. "Noooo… h-h-he was staa-aabbed." She finally got out hiccupping through her tears.

"Oh my." Amelia wasn't sure what to say.

Just then Becky came bustling in with two steaming mugs. "Ladies, here's your tea!" She plopped one down in front of Heather but took her time with… Amelia squinted to see her name tag… Sara. The youngest of the women just sat cradling the mug between her hands but not drinking. Heather, on the other hand, reached down into her handbag and brought up one of those tiny liquor bottles which she emptied into the mug. "That's better!" she pronounced to no one in particular.

Becky looked over at Amelia. "Ms. Feelgood, I'm glad you're back. I called the police of course, but they said it could be a few days until they can get here."

"A few days! What the heck are they doing?"

"We don't have police on the island. We've never needed them and we can't afford town personnel that we don't need. The worst crime that's ever happened here was when a couple of teenagers took a keg from the general store five years ago. Their parents sorted them out," she said with satisfaction. "For anything truly serious, we have to call over to the mainland but there's a bit of a jurisdiction problem."

"There is?" Amelia was fascinated. How could a place so close to a major city have a dead body lying around for days because the police didn't want to get involved? Then she thought of some of the alleys she'd seen from the bus in the city and reconsidered. But they wouldn't come right out and say they couldn't come. She looked around for another chair, but there weren't any so she took some of the bigger books off the shelf and made a perch for herself. She nodded at Becky. "Do go on."

"Well you see, a few years ago the legislature redrew the county lines for some of the smaller islands and we sort of fell off the page."

"They forgot you?"

"Sort of. The way I heard it we were supposed to be in one county but didn't fit on the legal-size printout and someone forgot to print page two. The person who wrote up the bill relied on the printed map. The adjacent county didn't expect us to be included, so they didn't. Anyway, they've promised to sort it out but it has to get passed by the legislature and you know what they're like. Nobody on the island has pushed it too hard because it keeps our sales tax lower and it's not like we ever got services from the county before that happened."

"How long ago was this?"

"About two years ago. It's not really been a problem until now. So anyway, the county sheriff can't come out here without it being in his county - I mean, he could but it's not in his budget. So, they have to argue about it with the state patrol and probably draw straws."

"Really?"

Becky shrugged. "Who knows. But they did promise someone would be here. And," she gulped, "nobody can come on or off the island until they do."

"What!" Heather jumped up, a look of panic almost creating an actual expression on her face.

"That's right, Miss Hammond. Dispatch alerted the ferry system so it won't be stopping until the hold is lifted. The police will come by private boat," she added clearly for Amelia's benefit as Heather was now up and pacing back and forth.

"I can't be trapped here. The killer is still on the loose. I'm too pretty to be on a small island with a murderer!"

Amelia checked to see if she was serious. She seemed to be.

"Um. I'm not sure looks are his primary motivation. Not if he killed Tony."

"Tony was gorgeous!"

Becky and Amelia looked at each other and both clapped hands over their mouths just in time. Tony was—err, had been—about five foot seven with a decided beer paunch, and thinning dark hair he wore in a comb-over and little piggy eyes.

"You killed him, I'm sure of it." Heather pointed at Amelia.

"Me! Why would I kill him?"

"Jealousy. You wanted him all to yourself."

"Err, no. But if I had wouldn't that mean I'd kill you instead?" Amelia was genuinely puzzled by the blonde's logic and hadn't thought about how her question would be perceived.

"She's threatening me! You heard her. Call the police back right now and tell them to hurry!"

"I did not threaten you. And I didn't kill Tony. I haven't even seen him since I arrived."

She turned back to Becky. "When exactly was he killed?"

"We don't know. Sara went in to do room service about twenty minutes ago and found him," she answered quietly. "Um. Ms. Feelgood, as the owner of the hotel, you'll need to make a few decisions, like how you want to tell the rest of the guests."

"What? I don't own the hotel. Whatever gave you that idea?" Amelia cultivated her sense of flair, but even she didn't think it extended to being immediately perceived as a hotel baron. Or was that baroness?

"Because your name is in the county register after Mr. Lyle died. Old Mr. Lyle." she clarified.

"He owned the hotel?" Amelia was mystified. She'd had no idea. Tony's father, Basset Lyle, had been a smooth talker. He was old-school New York, but he'd been a gentleman at the heart of it. They had not discussed their personal lives beyond one short conversation where Basset had asked her where she'd grown up. "Portland," she'd answered. He'd nodded and that was that.

"Yes."

"And now you think I own the hotel?"

"Yes." Becky nodded. "The quarterly update of the tax records came through yesterday. That county thing I mentioned? It means we're at the end of the list for any transfers or sales because the official county auditor only does them out of the kindness of her heart. Well, that and she doesn't want to be caught with the five-year mess by the time we're officially back in the county. So, they get done when everything else has been handled for the quarter. Your name is now listed as the owner of the hotel."

"But wouldn't I have to sign something? Or been notified of a will?"

Becky shrugged. "I'm not a lawyer. I have no idea."

Heather stopped pacing momentarily. "I'm sure you killed him. You wanted it all, didn't you?"

"I didn't want anything. Except to get my pension, quit my job and move to France where I will take up a hobby. What, I don't know yet," Amelia expanded as though someone had actually asked the question.

"You stole it from Tony. Who are you to own this property? You must have been sleeping with him."

"Who? Tony?" Amelia was revolted at the thought.

"No, of course not. Tony had much better taste." Heather patted her blonde coif. "No, his doddery old dad. His eyesight was going, everyone knew. You took advantage of him."

Basset's eyesight had been stellar as long as she'd known him and she was pretty sure he'd been gay.

"No, I can honestly say I have never had a personal relationship with anyone named Lyle."

"I don't believe you." Heather sniffed. "Just wait until the police get here. They'll take you away and take the property away too."

Amelia was getting tired of Heather, but also somewhat nervous as to what the police would think when they arrived to find her name was on the property where a murder had occurred. Where her disliked boss was murdered.

"Maybe you should show me where it happened?" she asked Becky quietly.

"Oh, I can't, ma'am. I had strict instructions from dispatch to keep the door locked and let no one in or out of the room. To preserve the evidence, they said." Her eyes gleamed. "Just like on TV!"

Hmmm. That was annoying, but it was a fair point in that Amelia had never been in the room, so perhaps adding her DNA to it would not be a wise move at this point.

"I see. Well is there any way to see inside the windows? You know from outside?"

"I think so. The upstairs patio deck runs along that room. It depends on if the drapes were closed of course." She looked over at Sara, who was staring down at the mug of tea in her hands. "Perhaps we should just go look. I should make sure the door is locked from that side anyway."

"Good idea."

They left Sara sitting pensively huddled in the big chair and Heather still pacing in her pink tracksuit and went upstairs.

❧

Becky led Amelia up a set of narrow stairs that was off to one side of the old house. They twisted and turned up the inside of one of the turrets, but without any windows. They must have been the original servants' stairs. "This is what the staff uses for quick trips when things are busy," Becky confirmed. "It's the only non-room access to that patio." She stopped on a small landing that had a narrow door built into the paneling. "Through here." She pulled it open and went first. It led into a small utility closet with extra toilet paper rolls and the like and then through to another exterior door on the opposite wall. Becky opened it.

"Isn't it locked?" Amelia asked with some alarm.

"No, why? The patio doesn't go anywhere. It's not like someone can get to it from outside the hotel."

It made Amelia nervous for some reason. Maybe it was just big city jitters. Outside, the wind was blowing lightly but not unpleasantly. A low railing guarded the edge of the slate patio that filled the space between the two oceanside turrets. Four rooms had French doors that opened on to it. Cautiously, Amelia walked over to the edge and peered over. The rocks took a little longer to tumble into the sea here compared to her room on the far corner, but not by much. She stepped back quickly.

"It's the third one here." Becky gestured at a pair of doors. The drapes were open and Amelia could see the outline of a body on the floor. She'd never seen a dead body before, not in real life anyway. It didn't bother her as much as she'd expected. Becky, on the other hand, looked a little green. She'd pulled her sleeve over her hand and tested the brass handle on one of the doors. It lifted and opened out. "Oh, God!" Becky wailed and turned away.

Amelia, on the other hand, leaned in. Tony was rather peacefully arranged in the space between the bed and the French doors. Except for the spreading red stain on the front of his white dress shirt, he looked fairly comfortable. "Hunh," Amelia said to herself as Becky was as far away as possible, clutching her elbows and breathing deeply with her eyes closed. Amelia peered into the room as far as she could without stepping inside. Nothing looked out of place. There were a couple of stacks of paperwork on the small table in the corner. The wardrobe door stood open and Amelia could see a couple of jackets and a tux hanging there. A 'gentlemen's' magazine lay open on the bed's red chinoiserie coverlet. Amelia was struck by the similarity between the pose of the featured young woman and Tony on the floor, without the blood of course. She really wanted to get a look at that paperwork but she didn't want to risk going in and trying to step over Tony. Hard to explain that to the police given the strict instructions. Inspiration hit hard, though, and she reached into the pocket of her pink jacket she was still wearing and took out her cell phone. Aiming the camera at the table and zooming in as far as she could, she thought she just might be able to make out the top document if she could get it on her laptop later. Taking a few pictures, she looked back at Becky, who was still breathing heavily. "You okay?"

"No. But I will be. Now I know why Sara looked so bad."

"Well, I'm going to close the drapes. No need for everyone to wander up here for a gander. How do we lock the doors?"

"From the outside? With this key." Becky held up a large steel skeleton key like the kind used in the 19th century.

Pulling the ends of her sleeves over her hands, Amelia reached up overhead and pulled the red drapes together as best she could without actually touching them with her fingers. She was sure the police would understand when she explained, but why have to explain any more than necessary? She pushed the doors shut and turned. "Okay, nothing to see here. Can you lock up?"

"Of course. Thanks." Becky quickly inserted the key and gave it an expert twist.

Amelia reached over and tested one handle with her sleeve. It was locked tight. "Good. Is that the only key?" she asked curiously.

"No, there's one kept in the old pantry which doubles as a maintenance desk. The grounds crew needs to come out here daily in the fall to blow the leaves off. This one hardly ever gets used."

"Interesting."

They started walking back to the turret where they'd come from. Amelia couldn't see the door. "Wait, where's the door we came out of? It can't have just disappeared."

"No, of course not. It's just intentionally hidden. It's all about the symmetry, I was told. It's just here." She pulled and twisted a small latch and a section of the shingling swung out like a normal door would.

"Hunh. It's like one of those fancy refrigerators people cover with paneling. Even though everyone knows a kitchen has a fridge in it."

Becky looked thoughtful. "I guess you could look at it that way. Once you know it's here, it's fairly easy to see."

They retraced their steps back down to the library, but Heather had disappeared. Sara stood wrapped in the arms of a burly gentleman wearing a red and black plaid jacket.

"Hiya, Mr. Roberts. You can take Sara home now. Someone will give you a call when the police get here. Eventually," she added under her breath. The man nodded at the two of them and led Sara out of the room.

"Her dad," Becky responded to Amelia's unspoken question. "She's only seventeen. He almost made her quit last month when Mr. Lyle made a pass."

"He made a pass at an underaged girl?" That was a new low even for Tony.

"Yep. Didn't answer when she called out she was room service. Found him naked on top of the bed. Luckily, Ralph was just outside. He's her uncle. They both wanted her to quit, but she said she couldn't. That she needed the money for school."

"And you let her go back in today?"

"I'm not really the manager here. I'm supposed to be reception with a little bit of filling in for whoever is out. We had a general manager, but Tony fired him. Right after old Mr. Lyle died."

"But if he didn't own the hotel…"

"Exactly. But until yesterday, we all thought he did. It's certainly what he told us. Mr. Jain wasn't in a position to question it. Anyway, to answer your question no, nobody was happy about it but Sara needs the money. She's saving for college and jobs aren't exactly thick on the island. We all figured Mr. Lyle would be gone again after this weekend so Ralph agreed to kinda hang out in the upstairs hallway while any of the girls were doing the rooms. That's why he was so close when she screamed."

"Good grief and I thought life on an island would be mundane."

"It usually is."

Chapter 4

❦

It was hard for Amelia to grasp all the ramifications of Tony's death as the pair walked silently back to the front area of the hotel. He'd died... well, nobody knew for sure, but sometime that day. And now they were marooned until such time as some police force decided to come for a visit. The sound of people talking got louder as they got closer to the lobby.

Amelia and Becky came back through to the tiny reception area to find a small crowd of people surrounding Ralph and all talking at once. "If you'll just listen... Can I... We need to..." he kept trying to interject without success. Becky gave a piercing whistle that made all eyes turn to her. Amelia was impressed and wondered if that was hard to learn.

"What's the matter?" Becky inquired.

Ten voices responded. "That woman said..."

"We need to leave."

"We want to..."

And so on. Becky turned to Amelia and just waited.

"What?" Amelia was genuinely at a loss.

"They've heard something. Remember I said you needed to do an announcement? They're not able to leave the island."

"And you want me to...?"

"You're the owner."

Amelia was still unconvinced on that one, but she hadn't spent the last six years in personal brand management for nothing. "Excuse me!" she inserted as loudly as she could. "We would be ever so grateful for your assistance. Could you please return to your rooms until the police can finish?"

Becky tugged on her elbow and muttered, "It could be days!"

"And enjoy your stay."

"We're leaving," a stout woman with brassy hair arranged in large curls insisted.

Amelia saw the panic start to form in Becky's eyes. "I'm afraid the ferry service is suspended for police activity. Your extended stay is on the house. It's the least we can do." Becky gave a small squeak at this announcement. Amelia just shrugged. She was pretty sure she couldn't be the legal owner of the hotel and a few days wasn't going to bankrupt the place. Besides what else could she do?

The large woman wasn't done yet. "I heard there was a murder! We aren't safe here!"

"You are, of course, welcome to find other accommodation on the island. But the free stay is only available to current guests. We won't be accepting any new guests until ferry service resumes." Amelia was speaking completely off the cuff but it seemed to be working. The guests mumbled among themselves. She marveled at how many of them were easy to match up. A few couples were wearing matching jackets, but a great many just sort of looked like each other. Maybe not physically but in their demeanor and mannerisms. Amelia was suddenly grateful that she was single. The crowd began drifting off, presumably to check out their options or confirm what Amelia had just told them. Becky and Ralph both let out sighs of relief.

"There are still more guests."

"How many?"

"Ten rooms were due in today on the ferry, they won't be coming obviously. So that leaves twenty rooms plus the five guest cottages."

"Right. How about I write something up and you can deliver copies and maybe we'll post one in here?"

"Okay."

Amelia didn't want to return to the library. "Does that computer have Word or something I can write this out with?"

"Yes, I think so." Becky went behind the desk and logged in. Amelia went with her and peered over her shoulder. There was the complex looking booking system and a game of solitaire up on the screen. "Sorry!" Becky blushed a little and closed the game window. She minimized the bookings and pulled up the main menu.

"I can take it from here," Amelia said not unkindly. "Can you come back in ten minutes to help me print it?"

"Of course, Ms. Feelgood. I'll… I'll just be in the back."

Amelia was already deep into her carefully worded announcement. The trick was to sound informative but not give any real information away. Like that there was a dead body. But too vague and people would come hammering with questions.

"There! That does it," she announced to herself with satisfaction when she was done. It had all the hallmarks of an earnest politician's speech. "Becky!"

Becky appeared as if she'd been waiting just out of sight. "Can you print this now and take care of the deliveries?"

Becky looked at the screen, reading the document that was still up and smiled. "Okay. They'll still have questions, you know. I do wish Mr. Jain was here."

Questions from frustrated guests weren't going to help Amelia figure this out. "Is he still on the island?"

"I don't know. His wife had cancer. That's why Mr. Lyle fired him."

"Because his wife was sick? Why? The cost of insurance?"

Becky's shoulders sagged. "No, because he had to take so many sick days to take her to the mainland for appointments. Sometimes he didn't come back for a few weeks because he needed to be there and there wasn't time to come back and go again. We tried to cover for him, but Mr. Lyle found out. I don't know how. Fired him over the phone."

That was brutal, even for Tony. "Well, see if you can find out when you're done with this. If he's still here, I'm happy to have him back while we figure this all out."

The smile that spread across Becky's face was like the sun cresting to the tops of the mountains in the morning. "Yes, ma'am! I'm not sorry he's dead you know," she whispered.

If Amelia was honest, she wasn't either, but life might be simpler right now if he wasn't. Much simpler, she thought, as Heather wandered in aimlessly with her cell phone glued to her left ear as she whined, "But Michael! I'm not safe here. I think that woman killed him." A long pause was followed by, "I told you about her. The one that stole Tony's inheritance. He must have confronted her and she killed him to shut him up."

Amelia couldn't believe her ears. Heather really thought she had killed Tony! Did other people think that? Would the police think that? Heather exited reception to the outside driveway, still talking. Amelia was frozen in place behind the desk. Becky came back in with a stack of printouts. "All set. I'm going to start slipping these under doors."

"Becky, do you think I killed Tony?"

Becky looked startled. "Did you?"

"No! Of course not."

"Okay."

It was not the fulsome denial Amelia had been counting on. Absently, she closed the document she'd written. A small square red icon with white eyes caught her attention on the screen. Chouette was the application label. "Becky, what's this?"

"What?" Becky was just about to leave down the hallway.

"This Chouette thingy."

"Oh, that's the security cameras."

"Wait! You have security cameras? How come nobody mentioned them?"

"Well, they're not in the guest rooms!" Horror filled Becky's voice. "What good would it do?"

"Of course not, but where are they?"

"Oh well, there's one there." She pointed to the far corner where in the shadows Amelia could just make out something small attached to the ceiling. "And I think there's another one on that upper patio and maybe one or two on the trail to the guest cottages. I don't know if any of them are working. We never look at them. We've never needed to."

"Mind if I do?"

Becky looked a little uncomfortable. "Maybe that should wait for the police?"

"You're right. It probably should."

Amelia stepped out from the desk and acted as though she was going to follow Becky down the hall. When Becky headed upstairs to start the deliveries, Amelia nipped back. The screen was still unlocked. How could she go about seeing what was there at her leisure? She truly didn't want to destroy evidence, but it was becoming increasingly clear that time was of the essence.

Chapter 5

❧

Her mind racing, Amelia stood there, staring at the computer screen. It started to dim before her eyes. "Eep!" she said as quietly as she could while still letting the release valve vent on the adrenaline rush she'd just experienced. She quickly reached over to move the mouse. The screen burst back to life and she relaxed a little. She looked back at both doors and listened for footsteps. Nothing. Should she do it? And risk the wrath of the invisible police? It was that last part that made up her mind. Before she lost her nerve, she reached again for the mouse and double-clicked on the little icon, half waiting for alarm bells to go off. None did, but the screen quickly resolved to a fancy red and gray dashboard with four black and white camera feeds arranged in a grid. One of them showed her behind the desk. Crap! Now everyone would know she'd been in here looking. "Except that they don't know what you're looking at, sweetie. Just that you're at the computer in a hotel that you own!" her very rational internal voice pointed out. She looked around the screen - there was a prominent button Save to Disk. In for a penny, in for a pound, she figured. She clicked. A small window popped up asking for a date range, which cameras and a destination folder. She set the date for two days prior up through today, selected all the cameras and then was stumped. Where could she save the file? It did no good to save it to the computer. She hadn't brought hers to the island so that was out. Plus, she didn't have time to go to her room and get back again. Could she save it and email it to herself? Her bag bumped against her hip as she bent to stare at the small print on the screen. The file size was huge - almost a gig. Her free email service was never going to let that go through. She pulled open the desk drawer to see if there were any ideas there. Just a pad and a couple of pens. A few rubber bands and some small change. Absolutely nothing technical or helpful.

She needed a thumb drive. Amelia was not particularly tech-savvy, but she'd learned about USB drives when Tony had started snooping in everyone's computers. Somehow, he'd gotten an admin override from IT and started looking around at everyone's files. He'd never explained why but started bringing things up in her one on one meeting like why she wasn't done with a particular report that 'should be easy' and how she was taking the wrong approach with the MacPherson account and so on. It had gotten so bad she'd finally gone and found Alex, whose permanent case of acne and stained t-shirts always made her uncomfortable. It was a bad look for teenagers, and on a forty-year-old man, it bordered on weird. But Alex had been strangely helpful. She'd only had to ask if there was a way to keep her files private until they were ready to share and he'd handed her a strange little silver bar and showed her how to use it. His eyes had lit up with an odd flame of excitement. Creepy and weird. But it had solved her problem with Tony, mostly. After she started saving her files to the drive and taking it home with her at night, he'd only been able to micromanage from the standpoint of asking her why she hadn't started yet. She'd held her ground and started marking up her desk calendar with how many more days she'd had to put up with him.

Amelia was diligent in always putting the small thumb drive in the coin section of her wallet. She always paid for purchases with plastic, so she never really had change to put there. It seemed like a secure hiding place because technically taking client files off-site was against company policy. Even though taking her laptop home wasn't. She hadn't dared ask how the two were different as Tony was clearly looking for any excuse to bully her into submission. She absently reached into her bag for her wallet without even thinking about what she was feeling for. When she unsnapped the coin pouch, she realized her subconscious was smarter than she was. There lay the shining silver bar with a pink ribbon threaded through the loop on the end. She had exactly what she needed.

She quickly found the one USB port in the ancient-looking computer and inserted the drive, clicking its location and OK on the little window almost simultaneously. A progress bar started to tick off the process very slowly. Amelia could hear Ralph and Becky chatting as they came down the hallway. She looked around frantically and then realized that the external drive was so small that they wouldn't be able to see it as long as they didn't see the screen. She minimized the window and forced herself to walk away from the desk and over to the rack of colorful tourist brochures.

"Oh, Ms. Feelgood! I didn't know you were still here. Did you need something?" Becky sounded a bit anxious.

"No, no. I don't really feel like sitting in my room and with the wedding off and all…." Her voice trailed off as she thought about the mess one dead guy could make of things. "I thought I'd just hang around and wait for the police to show up. You did say it might be a while but surely they'll find someone?"

"Oh um. They could but… well, it's not very likely. Maybe you'd like to see some of the local sights? There's a farmers' market every weekend and my friend David does a haunted house tour Friday and Saturday evenings in the summer."

"I didn't know the island was big enough for farms."

Becky looked a little embarrassed. "Well, um, it isn't really. A few people sell salad greens from their garden. And there's some produce that a few people bring over from the mainland but mostly its stuff people have made here from wild things like blackberry jam and Wild Bill Logan makes mead from his honeybees and then there's lots and lots of crafts."

"Oh. How lovely." Amelia was trying hard to not be rude and knew she was failing miserably. She went for a change of topic instead.

"And you have ghosts too?" Were these also brought over from the mainland? she wondered snarkily but managed to keep the thought to herself. If it showed up on her face, that wasn't her problem.

"Have you seen the village yet?"

"I think so. I had lunch at the vegetarian cafe."

"That's not the village, that's just a cluster of old buildings that didn't quite fit in the village."

Didn't fit? Amelia was beyond confused now.

Becky reached over to the brochure rack and plucked one out for Historic Findlater Village - Experience historic Europe through authentic architecture. She pointed to a black and white oval portrait of a man with a small mustache in a tweed suit. "That's Mr. Evans. He inherited the island after the first world war. He went over to Europe and bought whole buildings that people didn't want anymore and shipped them back. He created the village to have examples from every style and class of society so Americans could have an authentic experience without having to travel."

Amelia was doubtful as to how tearing down and rebuilding random structures gave an authentic experience, but it was clear Becky bought into the vision. If she could keep her on a roll the file could finish downloading.

"So, the ghosts came with the buildings?"

"Exactly. David says there are at least five real ones and he usually makes up one or two more for effect."

"But there's no bus or taxi, right? Walking back from lunch just about killed my feet otherwise I'd love to give your friends' tour a try."

"Oh, you can borrow one of the golf carts. We have ten for guests to check out for that very reason."

They had golf carts. Her blisters were completely unnecessary. Amelia bit her lip, hard, and looked down at the map on the brochure. "So, point me in the right direction. Where do I find him and where's the farmers' market? Maybe I'll take a quick walk through on my way to the ghosts."

"Well, we're here now, you see." Becky put her finger on some white space in the margin. "and if you take the main road past where you stopped for lunch and go about another five minutes, you'll come into the village here." She pointed again. "The farmers' market sort of spreads out from the medieval market cross here." She put her middle finger on a spot in the upper right quadrant. "It depends on the weekend and the weather. Sometimes it's small and sticks to the immediate area and sometimes, like a holiday weekend, it spreads out down the side streets. And then David starts his tours at dusk in the cemetery, here." She put her index finger on a point in the lower-left quadrant.

A weird thought entered Amelia's mind. "The cemetery wasn't also brought over from Europe, was it?"

"No, of course not! It's all locals. This isn't Brigadoon. People have been living here since the 1880s. It's not big. More people leave the island than live here permanently." And some like Tony left very prematurely indeed. Amelia couldn't stop the shiver that hit between her shoulder blades. She took the brochure from Becky. "Thanks. That's my afternoon and evening planned. Where do I find the golf carts?"

"They're just 'round the side over there. Ralph can help you."

"Great. I'll just change my shoes first, I guess." Amelia really just wanted to retrieve her thumb drive from the computer and head into the village. She'd spotted a library on the little hand-drawn map and maybe they'd have a computer she could use. She made as if she was going to walk down the hall with Becky, but it turned out she didn't have to. "Is there anything else you need? My shift is over and I'm heading home but if you need anything, I'm happy to stay and help."

"Oh no! You've done more than enough. You should get some rest. I'm sure you'll be really busy when the police finally get here."

"Okay then. See you tomorrow, Ms. Feelgood!" Becky walked out the door, her ponytail bobbing.

Amelia watched her until she was out of view and then scurried back to the desk. The file was done copying. She hurriedly closed the program and pulled the drive out, re-securing it in her wallet. She looked around to make sure everything was as she'd found it. Her shoes were still hurting her feet but this was more important. She headed out the door to find a golf cart.

❧

Ralph was nowhere to be seen, but it wasn't hard to find the little check-out kiosk and the line of golf carts. Each one had a number sticker on the front windshield and there was a notebook in the kiosk where you could write your name and the time. She signed out the one nearest the exit. Getting in, she settled herself on the bench seat and placed her tote next to her. She'd never driven a golf cart before but then a few hours ago she'd never seen a dead body either. Apparently, it was a weekend to knock out a lot of firsts.

Amelia took to driving the golf cart like a duck to water. The secret, she decided, was to pretend that she was driving a classic 1940s roadster, preferably pale blue with cream interior. That way she took it slow and didn't focus on how ridiculous the beige cart with the inn's emblem emblazoned in navy on the canopy actually looked. As she tootled down the main road towards the village, she wondered what the other wedding guests were up to. Many would be staying home obviously, as they'd never intended to come until tomorrow morning anyway. And now, even if they weren't aware of the death, the fact that the ferry wasn't stopping would keep them away. But some had come to make a long weekend of it and she probably knew at least a few of them. Tony was slimy enough to not have a huge social circle, at least not one that lasted for very long, so most of his 'friends' were more work-related. She bit her lip when she realized that pretty much described her social circle too. But once she got to France, things would be different. She'd find a hobby and make friends around that, maybe join a book club or something.

Her sense of flair would attract like-minded people and she would finally have her tribe. And then she was going to relax somewhere in the sun, surrounded by vineyards or maybe lavender fields, old stone buildings and drink wine. Maybe eat some olives and local cheese with a fresh loaf of bread.

She'd keep her ultimate goal in mind when she got to the farmers' market. Rather than look for crafts to buy (so not happening!) she could shop for a hobby. Talk to the crafters about how they'd got started and maybe find an introductory project. She fancied seeing herself as some sort of artisan in the future. Not one that needed to do it for the money, but one with skill and knowledge (and patience) to make lovely things.

As soon as she saw a parking space for the golf cart, she took it. Getting out, she settled her skirt where it had rucked up slightly and set off on her discovery tour. She found the edge of the farmers' market a few minutes later. White tents in various shades from clinical to dingy were arranged in relatively neat rows with a few thrown in to cover odd blank spaces. Some had just a top with the sides rolled up and some had gone for the full festival experience with just the opening pulled back. A few of the stands were starting to pack up slowly so she got out her phone to check the time. 5:35! Where had the day gone? She hadn't even thought about dinner yet. But now that she was, she was feeling a little hungry. She walked along the stalls headed to the core of the market. She could ask someone there for a recommendation. Google said dusk today was at 8:45 so she'd have some time to wander and eat. It had also said the market closed at six, but clearly that was a very flexible six.

The stalls more towards the center weren't as eager to leave. They were clearly getting more foot traffic and it was also becoming obvious that more than a handful of wedding guests had splurged for the full weekend. Where were they all staying? She tried not to stare as she wasn't in the mood for any lengthy conversations but it would be helpful to know who was on the island. Heck, maybe the killer was at the market right now? Amelia felt a thrill of excitement trickle down her spine. Definitely, she needed to blend in then and not attract attention. She slowed her pace to a tourist meander and fished in her bag for her big floppy blue hat. It folded up without losing its shape and was perfect for this kind of occasion. And even though it was still cloudy with a slight threat of rain she fished out her extra-large sunglasses and put them on too.

She started looking at the contents of the booths more carefully and paused in front of one that caught her eye. A woman was selling absolutely gorgeous quilts, some traditional patterns and some that were more like stained glass with fabric. "Did you do all these yourself?"

"Oh no, dear. We have a group. We take turns manning, or should I say womanning the stall." She pointed to the sign on the corner of the folding table that said Findlater Quilting Society. Amelia looked her over carefully. She was somewhere in her sixties with a trim but comfortable figure and wearing a lavender sweatshirt with a kitten on it outlined with pink rhinestones.

"Well, they're lovely."

"Thanks, we always like to hear that."

They mutually agreed without sharing that there would be no purchase. Amelia wasn't sure she wanted dinner recommendations from anyone wearing kittens, at least not until she'd checked out the other candidates. She looked again at a small wall quilt of soft green willow leaves trailing down and felt a brief spurt of envy. It would be nice to be able to create something so beautiful. She passed by two women in crocheted ponchos selling crocheted toilet paper covers and a man in denim overalls with duck decoys. The next booth was a woman selling fudge and Amelia swooped in on the free sample plate. The fudge was okay but the freeness deserved a thank you. "I so shouldn't have done that so close to dinner. I don't suppose you could recommend any place close to here?"

The fudge maker, a woman of about Amelia's age with green eyes and freckles, smiled. "There's a couple places right around the square.

A Chinese place over there." She waved generically through the tents. "And a sandwich place on that corner, but most everyone ends up in the pub." She half turned to point to a building that not only looked like a classic British pub that could be featured on any self-respecting BBC mystery but was actually a pub. The quaint hanging sign said it was The Hanged Man.

"Is that really its name? The Hanged Man? A bit grisly, isn't it?"

"Yeah, well sort of. I think the name on the receipts is Joe's Bar and Grill, but everyone calls it The Hanged Man because really, with that sign what else would you call it?"

"You could change the sign?" Amelia pointed out.

"Nope. The whole village is under historic covenant. Plus, most of us are tenants anyway."

"Oh, do the owners live on the mainland then? Or how does that work?"

The woman looked Amelia over. "Most tourists never take the time to ask. It's all one owner or most of it. I'm not sure who it is now but it's all what was Mr. Evan's estate. The guy that brought all these buildings here."

"Oh." Amelia knew she'd already asked more questions than she should have if she didn't want to draw attention to herself. So she said, "Thanks for the dinner info," and moved on. Hanging towards the back of the crowd, she did a quick circuit just to see what else there was to see. There was a pottery stall with some pretty jugs, and the requisite fruit and veg, but as Becky had already told her that it was imported. Since she didn't even have a kitchen here there really didn't seem to be any point in looking more closely.

Amelia felt a light tingle on her shoulder blades as if someone were watching her. She stepped into a tent that had the sides down just so she could discreetly look back without being seen. Crap, it was Mr. Martin and his pompous wife. They owned a bathroom tile business in Seattle and put a lot of money into marketing with Lyle Communications. Why, Amelia was never quite sure, as none of it made a jot of difference in their market share. Maybe they just wanted the tax write off? They were both looking in her direction before finally turning away and walking between the stalls towards the road. Amelia breathed a sigh of relief and turned around to meet the inquiring gaze of the stall owner. He was tall and lanky with brown curly hair and thin wire glasses. "Avoiding someone?"

"Not exactly, just not in the mood for conversation."

"Seems to be a lot of that going on," he replied enigmatically. Amelia waited for him to elaborate but he didn't. She did not want to draw any more attention to herself.

"What do you make?"

"Um, wood?" He waved his arm around at the display which did indeed feature turned wood bowls and vases.

She supposed she should have really looked before opening her mouth. Maybe the people-related questions would have been a better direction. But too late now. "Oh yes, how foolish of me. Please excuse me." And she left. Hopefully, she wouldn't have to see him again. Amelia hated feeling stupid. Even though the guy hadn't gone out of his way to be condescending, he'd looked generally confused that the answer wasn't obvious. Which was the precise problem. How stupid did it make you if you couldn't see he was selling wood?

Maybe it would be better to go get some dinner. Particularly if half the stallholders headed there after they packed up (it was just a guess, but she would do that if she had been sitting there all day talking to tourists.) That way she could be sure to avoid the Martins and the wood guy.

Decision made she tromped across the square through a narrow passage between two tents, jaywalked across the empty road to the pub and opened the door.

❧

The old and heavy oak door moved silently on well-oiled hinges. Inside it was so dim that Amelia could barely see, even when she remembered to remove her sunglasses. While she waited for her eyes to adjust, she let her other senses capture the scene. There were people here, but not crowds, and the conversations were family chats rather than drunken sports monologues. There was an old-world scent from centuries of beer being spilled on the old wooden floor with a lingering note of fresh grease. No veggie chips here. When she could finally look around, things pretty much matched up. It was still really dark and atmospheric. She wondered if this was on the ghost tour? A handful of people were hanging out at the small bar in the center of the room, more of a cutout window to the kitchen than a traditional bar, and about twice as many people were dotted around the tables. Amelia looked around and spotted a small table tucked into the corner behind the door. Perfect. She could see who came in but hardly anyone was likely to turn around and look her way. Plus, the corner was even gloomier than the rest of the establishment. She took a seat and swept off her hat, folding it neatly into her bag. Her dark hair would blend better with the shadows than the blue hat would. Her inner mind pointed out "you aren't really a spy you know or even a PI." She knew that but there was really a killer on the loose. And no police. She pulled out the small menu from between the glass salt and pepper shakers and took a look. There was a 'real' side featuring hamburgers, fish and chips, and the like and a tourist side that had 'wild boar sausage', Tudor salad and gooseberry fool. Amelia looked around the room and at the bulky guy behind the bar with a slightly squashed nose and a smeared apron tied around his thick waist. She turned back to the hamburger side of the menu.

When a young woman came her way with a pen and pad in her hand, Amelia was ready. "Fish and chips please, and a hard cider."

"On tap, or bottled?"

On tap?" She guessed that sounded better somehow.

"Sweet or dry?

"Dry." When had cider turned into so many choices?

The girl just wrote and nodded. "Be ready in a few."

Amelia went back to looking over the crowd. It was about what you'd expect. A few tables were clearly tourists. A few others were locals wanting to get out of the house on a Friday night. In the corner opposite Amelia's, on the other side of the door, sat a lone man with a clean-shaven head wearing clothing dark enough to completely blend into the shadows. She couldn't tell if he was wearing all black or not, but it was difficult to see where his body ended and the wall began. He looked up and over her way with stunning aquamarine eyes. She looked away quickly. She'd been staring and despite the beautiful color of his eyes, she didn't think he looked like someone you wanted to be caught staring at. He looked like an assassin. Or at least a TV assassin. She wasn't entirely sure what a real one looked like. Maybe he was famous? She bent over her bag so she could look up at him through her lashes. If he was famous, she didn't recognize him. He'd gone back to looking at his phone. Amelia rifled through her bag, not really looking for anything but taking occasional peeks at him. She still couldn't see much more than his bald head.

The waitress brought a loaded plate over to the man and took his empty beer glass away. He put his phone down and Amelia quickly diverted her attention to the other side of the room. She felt his gaze on her and felt a shiver of unease. She was fine. She was in a public place and he would have no way of knowing who she was. She was going on the ghost tour after this and there would be plenty of people about. He definitely did not look like the type that did ghost tours.

A few minutes later her food arrived and she did her best to put the man out of her mind. She was ravenous and had only just realized it. She glanced at the time on her phone. 6:45. The chips were thick wedges of Idaho potatoes that were crispy and hot, one bite off the end and she could see the steam curling up in the darkened room. And after dressing the fish with tartar sauce and extra lemon, it didn't disappoint either. She savored the coating of thin hot grease and fresh white cod.

The waitress came by. "Everything okay?"

"Delicious. Oh by the way, do you know what time the library closes?"

"Oh, it's been closed for days. It's only open on Wednesdays and Saturdays from ten to two."

"Good grief, that's not much."

The waitress shrugged like what are you going to do? It clearly didn't bother her too much.

Now Amelia had another two hours to kill and a scary man to avoid while she did it. She slowed her eating pace. More people started coming in and suddenly the place was packed. Amelia couldn't see the creepy guy because there was now a cluster of people just inside the door waiting for tables to open up. She glanced at her phone again. 7:30. She supposed she'd pushed it here as far as she could. She paid the check and went outside. Surprisingly, there was still quite a bit of daylight left. The market was empty but the tables and tents were still up. It made sense if everyone were coming back tomorrow to leave what you could. It looked eerie though, as if people could be hiding behind flaps as she'd done earlier. She stood on the sidewalk and took the brochure out of her bag, checking her position with the tiny map. It looked like she needed to go up the street, turn and come down back towards her starting point. There just wasn't a cross street which would have been the sensible thing to do. Amelia was starting to wonder about Mr. Evans and his made-up European village. She shivered a little, standing still on the sidewalk. The sun was low enough that it was no longer providing warmth and a little breeze had kicked up. She took a second to zip her jacket. A fair number of people were strolling about checking out shop windows and generally enjoying the early evening so she found the church and its cemetery without feeling that funny tickle between her shoulder blades again.

The church looked like it definitely pre-dated Mr. Evan's European fantasy. It was a small wooden box painted white with a simple steeple in the center front and a bell. The cemetery that swept to one side was equally basic. Classic rounded granite tombstones were arranged in rows, most of them leaning to one side or the other. One or two more modern, laser-cut examples were dotted in between and a low stone wall separated it from the road. Five or six people were already sitting on the stone wall waiting for the tour to start. Amelia saw a sign with someone at a cash box by the path and went over to buy her ticket. "One, please," she said when the person in front of her moved to find a place on the wall. The man with the cash box took a ticket and said "ten dollars" as he looked up. Oh no! It was wood guy. He turned wood and followed ghosts? It was too late to turn away. That would be even more embarrassing. If he recognized her, he didn't show it, so she dug a ten-dollar bill out of her wallet and handed it over. Then she went as far away as she could without making it obvious and sat down on the wall to wait.

A large woman with dyed red curls and sparkly tennis shoes came and sat down next to Amelia. "Oooh, I'm so excited. Have you done one of these tours before?"

"No, I haven't."

"Do you think we'll see any real ghosts?"

"No."

The woman deflated as if Amelia had stuck a pin in her side.

Now she felt mean. But come on, even if ghosts existed, which didn't seem very likely would they come out on cue twice week, every week? Amelia sure as heck wouldn't. If she were a ghost, she'd have her sights set on some very specific people and focus on making them extremely uncomfortable. She made her escape when the wood guy—what had Becky said his name was, David?—called out, "Any early birds are welcome to check out the church before we get started. There are unconfirmed rumors that the first minister still says his sermon on sin from the Prohibition era every Friday night. Only those with the sight are likely to be able to hear him, though."

The woman next to Amelia jumped up with a squeal of glee, gave Amelia a dirty look and hurried into the church. Amelia, on the other hand, having remained where she was, saw David press something on his phone. Chatter from within the church suggested that most of the tour so far possessed the necessary qualifications to see ghosts.

An older couple had also held back. They looked like they were at least eighty and since both of them had canes, it seemed likely that they were just reducing their walking, but they smiled politely at Amelia, who made an effort to smile back. Maybe she should have hung out in her hotel room after all.

When the tour finally started for real, Amelia found it easy to hang to the back of the small group as they walked back and forth across the village. They made a stop at an Irish cottage supposedly haunted by a sheepdog and a windmill said to possess the spirit of the last miller who died between the giant stones. The crowd gasped with ghoulish glee as they looked down the shaft now covered with plexiglass and dramatically up lit. Then it was on to the pub where David led everyone up a set of exterior steps to the area over the bar. It was a large empty space except for a small desk in the corner that held a CD player. Luckily someone else asked about it so Amelia didn't have to. "What ghost needs a desk and a CD player?" a middle-aged man asked as if he were starting off a stand-up routine.

"Oh, they use this space for dance classes in the mornings. If it runs late into lunch, then the pub just tells its patrons it's ghosts instead of ballerinas." Everyone giggled but then David lowered his voice. "The real ghost only comes out at night and only then if there are only believers present." The fat lady turned around to glare at Amelia. She shrugged her shoulders back in response. David didn't seem to notice, having taken his phone out again. Amelia began to wonder if there was an app readily available for ghostly apparitions. She'd have to check; it could come in handy.

Sure enough, a greenish-white light started to glow in a dim corner under the rafters. Amelia had had enough. While everyone's attention was on the 'ghost' she slipped back down the stairs and went to find her golf cart.

Chapter 6

❦

It took Amelia fifteen minutes to find the switch to turn the headlights on. After ten she almost gave up and thought about driving back to the inn in the dark, but visions of her somehow managing to drive off the cliff made her stop and reassess. Finally, she found the little button that turned on the low powered lamps at the front. She hopped in and set off down the road. The road was eerily quiet except for random thrashing in the dense woods at the side in the area between the hodge-podge of buildings and the village. It was considerably colder and since the golf cart didn't have sides, she was feeling the effect of the weather. Her lights caught the streak of a brown leg. Only a deer. She slowed down even further. She knew who would win in a contest between a full-grown deer and a golf cart. An owl hooted long and low, making Amelia jump on the bench seat. What would this be like if she'd waited until the end of the ghost tour?

Pulling into the little parking corral for the golf carts at the side of the inn, Amelia breathed out a sigh of relief as she turned off the ignition. She got out and stretched her legs before deciding that signing the cart back in could wait for the morning when she could see what she was doing. Opening the entrance door, she heard the faint ding dong of an electric bell as she headed down the hall and up the stairs. She was more than a little surprised to see the door to her room ajar. A furiously whispered conversation was underway so she leaned closer. Had the murderer returned to try to do her in as well?

But if so, why were they still there?

"Stop worrying. David assured me the tour would not end before eleven. He said he'd pull out the special extra ghost at the gas station at the end of the village if he had to.

"I don't trust him to manage anything that simple."

"How could he mess that up?"

"It's David. Now, what exactly are we looking for again?"

"I told you, anything that indicates what side of all this she's on. Papers, maybe a receipt. We'll know it when we see it."

"Great. One of those."

"Look under the mattress."

Amelia's jaw dropped in shock. People were searching her room, looking for something to incriminate her for what? The murder? She hadn't even been on the island, probably, when he'd been killed. She put her hand on the door to push it open and confront them. Then she thought better of it. Maybe they had a weapon. Maybe these were the murderers. There wasn't anything valuable in her room. Well, except for the vintage beaded dress, but even that wasn't worth dying for. Maybe she'd better leave them alone until they left. Then she'd get Becky to make her a new room key. She retreated farther down the hall where it split into a T and ducked around the corner. There was a ceiling light directly over the intersection, so she didn't think she could leave her nose hanging out around the corner without being spotted. Instead, she leaned against the interior wall and periodically did a quick dash of her head to see if anything had changed. Other than making herself a little dizzy and getting the beginnings of a crook in her neck, nothing happened for about twenty minutes.

On her last peek, she saw two figures just beginning to descend the staircase, but they were both dressed in dark baggy clothes and she couldn't see any distinguishing characteristics. She headed down the hallway. Her room door was shut as if nothing had happened. She paused for a long second and then continued down the hall.

She sped up, going down the stairs but by the time she got to the bottom they'd disappeared. Taking a deep breath, she slowed her pace to normal and continued into the foyer. A man was standing in front of the desk. His bald head caught the light, drawing her eye up. He was tall and dressed all in black. Slim black jeans and a black sweater. Was that cashmere? Becky came out from the back just as Amelia came into the room. Her hair looked a little mussed, but her uniform was the same blue one as before so if she'd been in Amelia's room, she was good at changing very fast. The man's head swiveled in Amelia's direction. His aquamarine eyes met hers and narrowed. He didn't smile. Amelia froze. It was the creepy guy from the pub. Had he followed her here? Had he searched her room? But if he had what was he doing waiting in the foyer?

Becky cleared her throat. "Can I help you?"

"Yes. I'm Gus Johnson. Sheriff Harrison asked me to stop in and look at the murder scene?"

"Umm. Let me just see if he left any messages." Becky turned to go back through to the back. "Becky!" Amelia wasn't going to be left alone with the man plus she didn't think he should get to see the crime scene before the police if she couldn't. "What is going on?" She shadowed Becky so closely that it would have been hard to get a piece of paper between them as they headed back to the small kitchen area that also served as the working office. "Who is that guy?"

"Gus Johnson, apparently. I've never met him."

"And you're just going to let him into the crime scene? What if he's the murderer?"

Becky closed her eyes and pressed her fingers to her temples. "I hadn't thought of that. I suppose it's possible, but why would he come to the front desk? Ugh. I shouldn't even be here but Tammy is stuck on the mainland. She went over for a dentist appointment yesterday and now can't get back so here I am again."

Amelia walked over to the answering machine - the light was blinking and there were two message slips tucked under the corner.

She picked up the pieces of paper first. One said 'call sheriff' and gave a number. The second said wedding - 20 rooms - 4th of July weekend - cost? and gave another number. She reached over and pressed the play button on the old-fashioned machine. The mechanical female voice said "you have sixteen messages. To listen to your messages press..." Amelia pushed the button again to make her stop and picked up the phone instead. Becky gasped. "What are you doing?"

"Calling the sheriff."

"Should you do that?"

"He asked us to, right? And you did say I own this hotel now?"

"Yeah, that's my understanding." Becky sounded uncomfortable.

Amelia pressed the digits for the phone number and listened to it dial. Then she heard that almost silent click as the call was forwarded, then it rang some more. Eventually, a very sleepy voice answered "Frank Harrison." It was not inviting.

"Um, Sheriff Harrison, right?"

"Yes, that's right. Who is this?"

"My name is Amelia Feelgood."

"Geez, another one? I told my brother to stop sending me strippers. It stopped being funny before it started. Sorry miss, but no."

He hung up.

Amelia held the phone away from her ear and stared at it. "Well, I never!"

"What?" Becky asked

"He hung up on me. He thought I was a stripper!"

"Oh well, I guess I can kind of see..."

"Do I look like a stripper to you?"

"Well um, maybe? I've never really seen one. The island doesn't really run to that kind of thing. But it's not like he could see you or anything. It's your name, you see." Becky took a couple of steps back as she spoke.

Amelia was dumbfounded and then she giggled. Surprisingly, nobody had ever pointed this out to her, perhaps because her classmates had been rather sheltered about things like stripper names and by the time she was in college, Amelia was nearly invisible to her peers, her flair being mistaken for unfashionable oddness until well after graduation.

"What now?" Becky asked.

"I'm going to call him back." And she did. She waited through the rings and the rings.

"Harrison."

"Mr. Harrison. I am not a stripper. What I am is the new owner of a hotel on Findlater Island currently containing a dead body."

"Oh, crap."

"Quite. Mr. Harrison. Now before I was so rudely accused - you are the sheriff, correct?"

"Yes, for the moment. Something tells me I might not get re-elected." He sounded resigned to that prospect.

"I don't think that's relevant at the moment. There is an odd man here claiming you sent him. He's not in a uniform and he's well, creepy. Did you send him?"

"Describe him to me." The sheriff had suddenly become all business.

"Um, guess he's about 6'2." Amelia raised an eyebrow at Becky for confirmation who shrugged and nodded.

"He's bald, wearing all black. Beautiful aquamarine eyes."

Amelia groaned and mentally kicked herself. Why had she said beautiful? That was hardly necessary for identity confirmation.

There was a choked laugh on the other end of the line. "Yeah, that's Gus."

"Why is he here?"

"I asked him to stop by and get a preliminary on the scene. Not exactly by the book, but it's going to be another day and a half before someone can get out there. Gus and I go way back. We did the academy together. Then he went on to... to a different career path. But he still knows the basics. I'd appreciate it if you'd let him take a look so we can get started on some legwork in the office."

"Another two days? Are you kidding me?"

"Day and a half tops. If I had an unlimited budget, then sure there'd be someone stationed there but normally they'd just be eating all the time because there's never been a serious crime on the island. So even if we had an officer there, they'd be out of practice."

"Well, how did he get here?"

"Didn't he say? He lives there."

"How do you know he's not the murderer?"

"Gus? 'Cause he's better than that."

Amelia could feel her eyes widen. He was better than what? She wanted to ask and didn't dare.

"Hey listen." The sheriff interrupted her panic attack. "Is Gus there? Can I talk to him for a minute?"

Amelia took the handset down from her ear again, stared at it and walked back into the foyer where the man, Gus, was standing semi-patiently with his legs spread and his hands clasped behind his back.

"He wants to speak to you," she said as she handed the handset over.

He took it without a word and raised it to his ear. "Frank."

Amelia could only hear one side of the conversation and most of it was happening on the other end. At one point, Gus's eyes cut to her startled and a slow grin spread over his rather chiseled lips. The laugh lines looked like they might just crack his face. He averted his eyes before saying, "I'll keep you posted, but I wouldn't hold your breath." He took the handset and found the off button before looking up. "Ladies, all clear? Shall we?"

Chapter 7

❦

Becky led the way upstairs, with Gus following behind Amelia. "Do you ladies mind giving me your names?"

Amelia wondered if the sheriff had mentioned that he'd thought she had a stripper name. She certainly wasn't going to bring it up. "I'm Amelia Feelgood." She paused when she thought she heard a muffled snort behind her. Gus didn't say anything, so she continued with just a touch of drama-applied frost in her voice, "and that's Becky Manderly."

They were at Tony's suite door. Becky took out her master key and inserted it in the door lock. "I'm surprised the police want you in here. They said before to lock it down."

"That would be standard procedure but think of it like I've been deputized, sort of. I can give them an initial report so they can do some basic research and fill in the blanks later. They've got my fingerprints on file so they can eliminate them. Which is why," he looked back at Amelia who had opened the wardrobe door, "you shouldn't touch anything." She shoved her hand behind her back and proceeded to stretch up on her tiptoes so she could maybe see the top shelf. It looked empty. Gus walked over to the far wall where Tony still lay on the floor between the bed and the wall. The room was definitely not smelling of citrus room freshener.

"Ms? Amelia, was it?"

"Yes. I'm Amelia Feelgood." She hadn't told him to call her by her first name but apparently, he wasn't a big fan of formality.

"Amelia, can you find the thermostat and turn on the air conditioning?"

"I'm allowed to touch that, am I?"

"Yes. Pretty sure this guy wasn't killed by or for the thermostat. Just set it as low as it will go."

Amelia turned to find the wall unit, grumbling under her breath. She found it and set it to the little blue dot on the left. Instantly, the room started to cool. Gus was still bent over the body and didn't look up. He took out his phone and took a couple of pictures and then returned it to his pocket. Next, he headed over to the table where the stacks of paper sat undisturbed from when Amelia had spotted them through the French doors. Now she could get a look too. She hurried over and looked over Gus's arm. He was using a pen to lift the edges of a few of the pages. "You were selling him this place?"

"What, no. I didn't even know I owned it until a few hours ago."

He looked at her disbelieving. "Well, he knew. These are sale transfer documents and what looks like a copy of the deed. More than this hotel, though. That map looks like most of the island."

Amelia looked over at Becky, who shrugged. "I only checked the assessor record for the inn. It didn't occur to me to check anything else. We can do that in the morning."

She maybe owned most of the island? For a lot of reasons, that didn't sound like good news. "What's the firm name on the top of the page?" she asked Gus. She'd have been able to see it for herself if he hadn't been hogging the edge of the table.

"Finchley & Patterson."

"Is there a phone number?"

"Sure," and he rattled it off to her. She put it in her phone and hit save. She'd call them first thing Monday and get this straightened out. It had to be illegal to just give someone an island without telling them about it.

Gus took a few more pictures around the room, poked his head into the bathroom briefly before saying, "Right, I think that's everything the deputies will find useful that I can provide. Ready to go?"

Amelia would have much rather lingered and gone through every drawer but was now more confused than ever so she followed Becky out and waited until Gus shut the door and tested the handle. "Right, thank you, ladies, for your time. I'll head out."

"Mr. Harrison said you live on the island. Where exactly?"

Gus turned around and studied her face. "Oh, over on the other side."

"What side is that? Don't you live in the village?"

"No, I don't. I live out in the woods. Why?"

"Because I saw you in the pub."

"Did you? I like a beer every now and then just like the next guy." He shrugged and opened the exterior door stepping out into the night without another word.

Becky started. "Ms. ..."

But Amelia held up a finger and just stood there and waited for a minute, but didn't hear a car engine or a motorcycle.

"Sorry, just wondering how he got here. What did he mean by the other side?"

"There are a few small places in the trees, but most of the island is either the village or Shin's Landing."

"Where's that?"

Becky grinned, "On the other side. It's northwest of the village - it was the servants' quarters for the big house and the construction workers when Mr. Evans put in the village and then later the staff and such when he was running it as an attraction."

"And do you think that's where Gus lives?"

"No. I live there and I've never seen him before."

Amelia felt her stomach tense. For such a small island there seemed to be quite a few mysteries. Not least of which was who had been in her room earlier. Should she have mentioned it to Gus? Or had he been part of that team?

☙

Amelia walked the short distance back to her own room, lost in thought and considering the two people that she'd overheard going through her things. She opened the door cautiously and turned on the light. A few things were slightly out of place, but not so she would have noticed if she hadn't already known someone had been in there. She turned on all the lights and took stock. Her fancy dress was still hanging in the wardrobe. She'd had all her valuables with her so there'd been nothing else to steal except the small wedding gift she'd bought already wrapped. She'd planned to re-gift the waffle maker her mother had bought off the shopping channel last year. She knew Tony didn't cook, but who cared? She hadn't wanted to be at the wedding. The wrapped waffle maker was sitting where she'd left it on the shelf in the wardrobe. She supposed she would now have to take it home. Heather definitely didn't look like she was interested in making waffles (eating them, sure).

It was nearly midnight but she wasn't feeling at all tired. Far less so than when she'd left the ghost tour in actuality. She piled up the pillows on the bed and sat down, reaching for the TV remote. Flicking through the twenty or so channels—apparently reception was a challenge on the island—she cycled through them again to see if something interesting had been hiding behind a commercial. It hadn't, so she settled for starting midway through South Pacific. She'd seen it at least ten times, so skipping to the middle wasn't that big a sacrifice. Then someone walked by her room and she jumped, her heart in her mouth. She got up so she could see the door. The handle wasn't moving and there weren't any more noises. Probably just someone returning to their room. She went to the door and cautiously opened it. She peered out cautiously.

Nobody was in the hallway. She shut it again and looked at the locks. There was an extra deadbolt, which she engaged, but it didn't look all that sturdy. She swiveled to study the room. She could drag the desk in front of the door, but it would obscure the bathroom entrance. She'd have to climb over the desk to get in. You're just jumpy. There's nothing going on she told herself as she went back to the bed and the movie. She sat down again. But then a commercial came on for home security that showed a woman cowering in a closet. She flipped off the TV. "That's it," she announced to the room. She might as well get ready for bed and then move the desk. Maybe that way she wouldn't need the bathroom until morning. She followed through on that plan, changing into her peach silk pajamas that she saved for traveling because they folded up so small, brushing her teeth and moisturizing her face. Moving the desk was harder than it looked. It was both dainty and solid. Eventually, she pushed it across the carpet and into position. Then she turned off the lights and got into bed, straining her ears for any suspicious noises.

❦

Invigorating sunshine was flooding through the tall windows. Yawning and stretching her arms over her head, Amelia contemplated the day. She still needed to get to the library and try to look at that video footage. And Becky was going to show her how to check the property records online to see if she really did own most of the island. Did she own Gus's place? Now that was a thought. She thought about the contrast between his eyes and generally grim disposition and grimaced. Perhaps he would stay out of sight now, presuming he really wasn't the killer. She wondered how long it had been since the sheriff had seen his old mate; maybe Gus had gotten clumsier in middle age.

And then there was the matter of breakfast. Still in bed, she eyed the fruit basket on the table. Someone had clearly undone the cellophane and attempted to refasten it but without too much skill. That didn't bother her but what if the mysterious room searchers had actually had syringes of poison and injected a banana or one of those juicy grapes. She could die and all traces would be gone before the police ever made it to this god-forsaken island.

Now thoroughly wound up, she got out of bed and dragged the desk back across the room. She would get dressed and go find Becky to dispose of the fruit basket and see what else she could suggest for breakfast. She showered and wrapped in one of the plush hotel bathrobes that had been hanging behind the door, returned to the bedroom to get dressed. It was then that she realized she only had one remaining outfit, the one she'd planned for the morning and to mix up for the return trip on Sunday Where did people on this island even buy clothes? Probably on the mainland, she realized sadly. Heck.

Still, she did have the one outfit, so she got dressed in white capris and a pink and white striped Breton sweater, grabbed the fruit basket and headed downstairs to find Becky.

Becky though, it turned out, had gone home. A very serious older man in a blue uniform vest explained this kindly. His name tag said Sydney. "I used to work here twenty years ago, but now with the um, incident, they called me in. They said 'Sydney, we need you. Can you help?' And of course, I said I would. Mind I'm not really sure where anything is anymore. Things do keep changing." Amelia eyed him suspiciously. She'd known a few Sydneys in her time. They were all lost in their own little worlds and it got worse with age. She looked at the fruit basket she was holding. If she gave it to him, he'd forget that it was meant for the trash and eat something, probably the poisoned banana and then it would be her fault. She'd better go find the Dumpster herself.

"Do you know where I can get some breakfast?"

"Hmmm? Oh no. I couldn't say. There used to be a restaurant here you know, back in the heyday. Everyone got dressed up, came over on the ferry for a night out. Those were the days."

"Well, where do you go now?"

"Hmmm?"

"For breakfast?"

"Oh, I have oatmeal at home."

"Every single day?"

"Yes, it keeps things uncomplicated." He smiled at her wistfully.

Amelia kept her groan to herself and just smiled, taking her fruit basket and her frustration out to the driveway. She'd need a golf cart again, so maybe there was a Dumpster over near the service area. There was and she even found a box to stand on so she could toss the basket in. She felt bad. Becky had clearly gone to some expense for it, but she couldn't trust it after people had been in her room.

She got down from the box and went and found the same golf cart she'd used yesterday. Since she hadn't checked it back in, she figured she didn't need to check it out again either. In seconds she was bouncing along on the way to the village. She kept going, past the little cluster of shops without slowing. She wasn't going to settle for lentil pancakes and chicory coffee, even if it was closer. No, she wanted the works with bacon and eggs. The pub seemed the most likely place to find them.

Chapter 8

❧

The pub was positively hopping with activity. This time there was only a locals' menu, which made Amelia wonder if they hadn't been able to come up with any merrye olde European offerings for breakfast. French toast was usually a safe bet in an unknown locale, so she ordered that and got her very own carafe of dark coffee. Things were starting to look up. And the library opened in half an hour and was just two streets over.

The Saturday breakfast crowd was very different from the Friday night customers. Small children were everywhere as were the thick plastic glasses of crayons meant to keep kids loosely tied to their table of origin, but it didn't really work. Either they all knew each other or were just really friendly. Kids were moving around the pub like gyrating electrons. Amelia had hoped for her corner table from last night, but it was occupied by two old women gabbing, so she stuck it out in her middle of the row table and tried not to eat too fast. As a child, Amelia had been what her peers referred to as a goody-two-shoes. She rarely had friends as she was too busy mentally preparing to become the first woman to circumnavigate the globe in a glider. At the time, nobody was interested in hearing about wind vectors over the Sierra Madres. By the time she'd let go of that dream, about age ten, she'd already been permanently labeled weird. As a consequence, even as an adult, children made her nervous.

That was unfortunate because most of these migrated with her from the pub to the library, with the ease that spoke of a long-standing tradition. Amelia waited for them all to file in when the door opened and then stood in line for the lone librarian's attention. The library wasn't very big, roughly about the square footage of her condo in Seattle, but it was neatly divided into diagonal zones, with a childrens' area by the windows and the checkout desk in the center. The librarian was a very patient woman in her fifties who calmly and pleasantly dealt with missing books, gave directions to the video section, and helped a young boy of about seven place a hold on a Star Wars book. By the time it was Amelia's turn, she thought she had a good gauge of the librarian.

"Hi, I'm on the island temporarily and didn't bring my laptop. I was wondering if there was a computer here I could use?"

The librarian's hazel eyes sharpened a little. "For anything in particular? We have one over there," she gestured to a little ledge that had been attached to the main desk, "for Internet access, but it's for fifteen minutes at a time and it's heavily child-guarded."

"Won't even let you shop for underwear," said a disgruntled voice behind Amelia. She half-turned to see a shrunken old woman with a cane and one of those clear rain hats tied under her chin. Amelia half nodded before turning back to the librarian.

"Actually, I just want to use this." She fished out her thumb drive. "I have a couple of files I need to check."

"No, sorry. We don't have anything for that. Too many viruses about - way beyond our budget."

Amelia hadn't expected to be turned down and hadn't prepared a plan B. "Well do you have any suggestions? It's not like I can leave to go home and get my laptop."

"Did you check with your hotel?"

"They don't have anything either." Well, they did, but that would defeat the purpose of looking at it privately.

"I don't know, really. You could check with the hardware store, maybe they have a cord or something?"

Amelia sighed. "Okay, thank you."

This was not going to get her anywhere. She went back outside and sat down on the pretty blue bench to one side of the front path. Flowers were blooming and the sky was a clear blue. There was a pleasant floral scent in the air that made everything truly feel like spring. She might as well sit here as opposed to inside to figure it out. She got out her cell phone. It had slightly more signal here than at the inn so she typed in computers to the map feature. There was no mention of the hardware store, but there was an electronics refurbishing establishment two streets over. Since the weather was so nice, she decided to walk.

She had to go back and forth on the street three times before she finally saw the tiny sign for "Electronics bought and sold" partly because the sign was genuinely tiny but also because it was housed on the top floor of the windmill she'd visited last night on the ghost tour. Somehow her brain just couldn't accept that a shop like that could be in anything other than a dingy strip mall. It violated some rule of the universe, she was sure of it. Amelia opened the main door of the building, smiling in response to the waved hello of the woman running the fabric shop on the ground level and started walking up the stairs. She didn't think to count them until she was at the top but it felt like she'd climbed six flights at least. When she got to the top-most landing, having passed a lawyers' office and a real-estate place midway, she was dismayed to see one of the little plastic clocks on the door that said back in ten minutes.

The worst part was she was sure it had taken her ten minutes to climb up there and nobody had passed her on the way down. Should she wait it out? She peered through the glass door and gave it a tug. It was indeed locked. There were a couple of desk lamps on towards the back. She would wait, then. That looked like a likely sign that someone intended to return.

She sat down on the top step and made herself comfortable, wishing she had a cappuccino to keep her company. Instead, she got out her phone and did some of her French lessons. She was almost through the basic level. She couldn't wait until she could discuss shoes in detail. There was no need to get sloppy with her goals just because she was now probably out of a job.

Eventually, she heard voices talking jovially down the stairs. The staircase was curved so she couldn't see who it was but it was clearly two men discussing football. Or was it hockey? Football didn't have nets, did it? But of course European football did, so now she was confused. Was at least one of them coming up here? She checked the time. She'd been waiting at least twenty minutes. Maybe it was time to try something else. There were still several items on her to-do list for the day.

But then footsteps came up the stairs towards her. Whoever it was was taking them two at a time. She wasn't surprised when she finally saw the gangly young man with a mop of auburn curls and glasses. His jeans weren't quite long enough to cover his ankles but his weather-beaten sneakers said he didn't care. He was smiling and carrying a cardboard drinks tray with just one tall cup.

"Oh hello, I hope you haven't been waiting long?"

"Well yes, awhile." She tried not to let the grumble out in her voice. "Google said you might be able to help me. I need a computer to work on some files since I can't get home to get to mine."

"Why not?"

"The ferry isn't stopping until the police get here, didn't you know?"

"Oh, I rarely leave the island. I don't subscribe to the ferry alerts, too much angst when the lines get long you know? If I'm not going anywhere, why do I need to know that there's going to be a delay?"

"Okaaay. Well anyway, someone was murdered and now nobody can come or go until someone in uniform finds some spare time."

"Hunh. Only time I've ever seen the police here was when they did one of those corporate leadership retreats." He laughed. "Good thing they weren't allowed to bring their guns. You've never seen so many irritated people."

"So, do you sell working computers or is there one I can rent?"

"Mostly I sell off parts of old machines on the Internet, mail them out at the post office in the morning and then I get coffee for everyone in the building on my way back."

"So, you don't have anything I can use?" She eyed his coffee cup with envy.

"Well I might, actually. This guy brought in a laptop yesterday. Wanted some quick cash. I gave him fifty for it because it's relatively new and that's all I had on me. As far as I know it works, so yeah, you can either buy it for one hundred or I'll rent it to you for ten a day. But no guarantees it doesn't have a virus or something. I haven't had time to check it. How's that?"

"What do you mean a hundred? You just said you bought it for fifty."

"I did, but that was spec, right? Now I've got an interested buyer so clearly I need a profit. This is a business."

"Seventy-five and you make sure it works okay before I walk out the door and that there's a power cord."

"Okay." He put down his coffee so they could shake hands.

Amelia grumbled to herself about highway robbery while Seth, as he'd introduced himself, turned on the small laptop to run some diagnostics.

She wandered over to the small window. Seth had an amazing view of town and out to the water. She could see small fishing boats dotting the calm sea. One of them was gradually moving towards the island.

She turned around to Seth who was bent over the laptop now connected with a cable to his bigger machine. "Hey, when they stop the ferry like this, what about the little boats?"

He glanced up. "One, it's never happened before in my lifetime. Not for the police. There was that time that a cruise ship took out the dock about ten years ago. And two, it's not a prison, people have the right to come and go just like anywhere else in the country. Can't see anyone telling islanders they can't use their boats. Not without it being something like nine-eleven, you know?"

"So, the murderer could have already escaped."

Seth shrugged his shoulders. "You're the first person to tell me someone's been killed. Must have been a tourist?"

"Sort of." Amelia still wasn't clear on Tony's relationship to the island, or hers for that matter.

"Islanders don't mix with tourists too much unless they're catering to them somehow. It's different when you spend winters here. The tourists just come and go, wander through the quaint buildings and buy souvenirs made in China. What's the point?"

She didn't have a rebuttal for that one. Luckily, Seth was done. "It's all good, a fairly expensive machine really. You're getting a deal." This boy was wasted on the island. He'd be running some unicorn startup if he lived in Seattle. He threw in an old computer case and luckily was able to process her credit card. Now time to get back to the inn and see what the heck was in those camera feeds.

Chapter 9

❧

It occurred to Amelia as she slowly walked down the stairs of the windmill, clutching her new-to-her laptop that if she headed straight back to the inn that she would just need to turn around again to find some lunch. She still needed to call those attorneys from the land deeds, but it was Saturday and they were unlikely to be answering phones. So, first the tape, and then some lunch. Maybe she'd try one of the other restaurants. This was the part Amelia hated the most about traveling. You always felt that you needed to be out of the room, and yet nowhere else really had privacy or places to plug things in. It left her unsettled. What she really wanted was her own place, where she could fix a cup of tea and lounge on the couch as she watched the feeds.

She walked back towards where she'd left the golf cart with no particular destination in mind yet. The islanders running shops were all acting as normal as were some of the tourists, apparently the ones that had already been planning to stay the week and so weren't concerned about the ferry. Others were much more antsy. She heard one woman pulling a man out of the used bookshop by the back of his shirt. "Harold, you need to find out what they mean by police activity. Call someone, for goodness sake. You're an executive. Find out why the heck we're stuck here and poor Heather isn't getting married."

So, they didn't know about the murder. Wasn't Heather telling people? She'd been bawling about it loud enough yesterday. Amelia tried to stay behind the couple without being obvious that she was following them. It wasn't hard. Harold might have been an executive plumber, but he was no captain of industry. Dressed in beige chinos and a white off-label polo shirt, he blended into the background. His wife, on the other hand, was wearing orange capris and a magenta and orange flowered blouse. Her hot pink hat was so wide that turning her head was virtually impossible while she clutched Harold to her side. Otherwise, she'd take him out. Amelia watched her mince down the sidewalk in orange stilettos and wondered what she saw in the mirror. Did she think she had flair? Or had she bought the entire outfit off the shopping channel? Or maybe it was a bit of both.

"Ooh, Harold! Look. I've always wanted one of those." Harold and Amelia both looked. There was a little kiosk where the curb kicked out from the sidewalk. It rented bicycles built for two and included a free map of the island. Amelia smirked. And watched the back of Harold's balding head pale. "Mitzy...."

"Oh, come on Harold, it will be fun."

Amelia stepped inside a nearby shop, which turned out to be another used bookstore, while Mitzy went up to the kiosk window. In no time, she was on the back of a bike, seated calmly while Harold pedaled awkwardly up the street. Amelia thought she could see the beads of sweat starting to roll off his head already. While she'd been waiting for them to leave, she'd idly browsed the table of books in front of the window and realized she'd actually found one she wanted to read. Hobbies for the Busy Woman and it was on sale for $2.99. She took it up to the cash register, made her purchase and then casually made her way to the bike kiosk. There was no way she was going to exert herself like poor Harold, but she wanted one of those maps. She opted for the blunt approach, "Excuse me, but could I have one of those maps?"

"Well, um. I'm supposed to only give them to bike customers," said the teenage girl behind the tiny counter.

Amelia picked one up and flipped it over. "It says here Findlater

Tourist Board and I'm a tourist."

"Well yeah, but Mr. Jain has to pick them up at the information center in the ferry terminal and bring them back."

Amelia recognized that name. "Is that the same Mr. Jain that used to work at the hotel?"

The girl shrugged. "I dunno. I just work here."

"Then you won't mind sharing one of your maps since they're free to the public anyway."

"I guess, okay fine." She said it as if Amelia had just told her to clean her room with a toothbrush. She must be a joy at home. But she had her map so she turned away with a smile and perused her surroundings. In following Harold and Mitzy, she'd ended up in a part of the village she hadn't seen yesterday. It had more Germanic buildings, and what looked like a Swiss chalet with shops in the lower and upper levels. She shifted the computer case to under her arm and pulled open the map. The Tourist Board had done a very thorough job. Bathrooms were clearly marked and shops and restaurants were listed in a directory on the back. Near where she was standing was a cheese shop, a bakery and some specialty import places, but no restaurants. The day had warmed up to where she was considering stopping somewhere to take off her jacket. Maybe she should just buy some supplies and have a picnic. She didn't need an Internet connection to watch the camera feed and she could go to that little park on the map and have some privacy while she watched it. Just in case anyone thought it was weird that she was watching security footage. As long as she didn't sit too far back in the trees where the murderer could get her, she should be fine. Mind made up, Amelia headed first to the cheese shop and bought some aged goat cheese and olives and then across the little breezeway between shops where she found a baguette and wonder of wonders, cafe au lait. The day was really starting to look up. She wondered how Harold was doing on his bike ride.

She took her bounty over to the little city park one street over.

It was about half a block in size with a few clusters of trees, an empty bandstand and a few picnic tables. Some kids were running around, but since there was no specific play equipment, they seemed to mostly be just working off steam. She claimed one of the picnic tables, putting all her bags on the top. First, she pulled out the laptop and found the thumb drive and the earbuds that went with her phone. She was pretty sure there wasn't any sound but she'd learned long ago that earbuds make a person look busy and like maybe you should think twice before disturbing them. Then she took one of the paper napkins the lady in the bakery had been kind enough to include and spread it out in front of her. She broke off a section of the baguette and a chunk of cheese and opened the loosely tied bag of olives. Someday soon she'd be eating like this in France every day, she was convinced of it. Before her fingers got too messy, she turned on the computer and queued up the video. It took her a few tries to decompress the file and then find where the files had gone but eventually, she found it in a temporary folder. There were actually five feeds listed, not just the four she'd seen on the inn's computer but the problem was she didn't know which was the extra. Not that it mattered, she needed to watch all of them. She got one going and figured out how to speed it up, then bit into the still-warm bread. It was heaven, crispy/crunchy on the outside and feathery light on the inside. As far as you could get from micromanaging, murdered bosses and lentils. She chased it with a green olive and a nibble of cheese, the salty brine tingling on her lips.

Absolutely nothing was happening in the first feed. It showed an empty path that led through the trees. Amelia wasn't sure where that even was but it must be somewhere near the inn. Something moved into view of the camera. A deer. It moseyed up the path, leaned in to eat some of the flowers and then meandered off camera. The feed went back to boring empty path. Amelia looked at the time stamp. She'd watched the couple of hours around when Tony must have been killed so she'd switch to one of the others and watch the rest of this one later. Maybe tonight when she couldn't sleep. The next camera showed the lobby. And there was almost too much activity. Most people had apparently left and arrived around the time that the foot ferry came in a few hours before Amelia arrived on the car ferry. Becky was going back and forth between checking people out, who then left the lobby with suitcases, and checking people in. She didn't see Tony or Heather; maybe they'd arrived the day before. She did see a tall solidly built man come in and talk to Becky, who picked up the phone. He had a tattoo on his lower arm that extended slightly to the back of his hand. He didn't check in or out, just waited for her to get off the phone and say something before he turned and went through the arch towards the staircase upstairs. He stood out because absolutely everyone else was paired up. Some were two women together, whether friends or partners wasn't clear, and then men with women of all age combinations.

"How odd that that's odd," Amelia said to herself. She watched for a while longer, still eating her bread and cheese before switching to the third camera. This one showed the garbage Dumpster and the golf cart corral. It also didn't have much activity, but she did see Heather check out a golf cart and drive it away. Was it strange that she was by herself? But then she wouldn't be with Tony on the day before her wedding most likely. She was wearing jeans and a t-shirt that showed off her considerable assets, not the sweatsuit Amelia had seen her in later. An older couple took a golf cart and took about twenty minutes just figuring out how to drive it out of the corral. Amelia rather thought that was the comic relief of the video. At least she'd done a little better than that. Then Heather came back just before 1pm, parked and dashed away as if someone were after her. If she signed the golf cart back in, Amelia couldn't see because the camera lens didn't go that wide.

The fourth camera showed the view down the hill towards the ferry. It didn't look like much use unless a rock climber had murdered Tony because there was no road or path visible. Maybe someone had moved the camera? Or bumped it? She didn't spend too much time on it, deciding instead to open the fifth one. This could make or break her investigation.

"Jackpot," she said under her breath when she saw that the footage was of the upstairs hallway. Just then someone tapped her on the shoulder. She twisted around while slamming down the laptop lid. It was Gus. He waited for her to remove the earbuds.

"What do you have there?"

"Nothing, just some videos for work." Half lies always work better than full ones in her experience.

"I thought you were in communications?"

"How do you know that?" Two could play at this game.

"It says so on your LinkedIn profile."

Oh yeah, that. "Video is very hot in communications these days."

"Hmmm. You wouldn't be concealing evidence, would you?"

"Absolutely not!" She wasn't. These were copies after all. The police were welcome to the originals if they ever got around to asking for them.

"And you wouldn't be trying to do a little sleuthing of your own?" He was smirking a little as if to suggest he already knew that's what she was doing and that she was unlikely to get anywhere with it.

"Either sit down or move back so I can get up. I'm not going to get a twisted neck talking to you."

"Fair enough." He sat down, straddling the bench of the picnic table, too close for Amelia's comfort. That had not been the option she'd wanted him to go for.

She decided to try another tactic. "When you looked at T...um the body, could you see how he died?"

"What do you mean?" His gaze sharpened.

"Well, clearly he was dead. And there was blood on his chest."

"How did you see that? You were on the other side of the room." His tone turned suspicious again.

"Becky and I secured the door from the patio side earlier in the day. It wasn't locked."

Gus swore under his breath. "Neither of you thought to mention that pertinent little fact?"

"Why would we? You didn't ask and you are not the police. Clearly. Because a good detective would ask about things like other doors, right?"

She could hear him grinding his teeth.

"So, was he shot or stabbed? Or something else?"

"Stabbed, and the knife was left under his body. It's probably not got prints or they wouldn't have left it," he said reluctantly. "Forensics will deal with it when they get here."

"Which is when, exactly?"

"Probably Monday."

Gus reached around her and took some olives out of her bag, popping them in his mouth.

"Hey! That's my lunch!"

"What, all of them? You've been sitting here popping them like pills for the last ten minutes at least."

He'd been watching her. And she hadn't had a clue until he put his hand on her shoulder. She needed to be a lot more aware of her surroundings, especially if there was a killer on the loose.

"Why are you here and why are you watching me?" she demanded with false bravado.

"You're entertaining." One of those smiles that seemed to crack his face open appeared like the sun after a rain shower. "The island is nice and all, but it gets a little… monotonous."

"So you thought you'd just follow me around?"

"I came in to get some new books." He nodded towards the backpack Amelia hadn't noticed until now. "Then I saw you. I've known some strippers, with and without stripper names, but I've never met a non-stripper with a stripper name. Was your mom a stripper or something?"

"It is not a stripper name!" Amelia was torn between outrage and the bizarre thought of her uptight, going to church three times on

Sunday, mother as a stripper. Her mind couldn't process it at all so she stopped. "It was my dad's name anyway and I promise you, neither he nor his parents who grew up in a Pennsylvania mining town were strippers."

"Hunh. Go figure."

Now it was Amelia grinding her teeth.

"Aren't you at all worried that there's a murderer on the loose?"

"Not really. There's usually one about somewhere, if you think about it. Clearly whoever was after that guy was after him specifically so that's a lot better than the average, just want to kill people, anyone will do type."

"It is?" Amelia couldn't really disagree. It was just that Gus was so matter-of-fact about it. It was weird. "How long have you been on the island?"

"Hmmm. Been about six months now. Starting to go a little stir-crazy, frankly."

"And you didn't know Tony?"

"Who? Oh, the dead guy. Nope never saw him before," he said cheerfully. "But then locals and the tourists don't mix much." He sounded almost exactly like Seth.

"I'm a tourist, you're talking to me."

"That's different."

"How?" she asked with dread.

"You're entertaining. You have a stripper name. And you think my eyes are beautiful." He smirked as he got up from the table. Amelia closed her own eyes in embarrassment, feeling the heat rise in her cheeks. Of course, that loose-lipped sheriff had shared her gaff. When she opened her eyes again (murderers were around after all), Gus was nowhere to be seen. She couldn't see him anywhere. She swiveled and nope, not there either. How had he done that? She could see down the street clearly from the little rise hosting the picnic table. Even if he'd run, she should still be able to see him. But nothing. And he didn't emerge from any of the shops either.

Clearly, the park wasn't private enough, so she'd better retreat to her room to watch the last camera and go over the others in more detail. She gathered up the remains of her lunch for later, maybe breakfast? She stowed all her purchases on the seat of the golf cart and headed back to the inn. Unlike last night, there were enough people out and about that she frequently had to stop and wait as nobody seemed to think anything of just wandering across the street at any old point.

Amelia had to stop again for a big group of tourists, the front part of the pack constantly turning to talk to the back half and all of them oblivious to her need to drive down the street. However, she decided it was a blessing in disguise because the delay occurred right in front of a wine shop with an empty parking space. As soon as the last of the people were out of the way, she zipped the golf cart into the spot. She left the food but didn't dare leave the computer in the open vehicle so she lugged it into the shop with her oversized tote bag. The proprietor, a middle-aged man with a slightly pompous haircut (Amelia suspected addictive use of product), eyed her bags and the nearby stacked bottle displays with alarm. That was okay with her she didn't really want to linger over discussions of bouquet and lingering oak notes. She'd once, long ago, briefly had a boyfriend that was into that sort of thing. She'd dumped him when she'd refilled one of his cherished bottles with cheap stuff from the grocery store (after drinking the original contents when he was out of town and she didn't want to get dressed to go to the store.) He hadn't noticed the difference. She'd even asked him if something seemed off and he'd gone on and on about her uneducated palette. She'd told him to pack up and leave that very moment. He'd seemed bewildered, but by then she didn't care enough to explain. This guy reminded her of Jeremy, a lot. So, she went for where she knew it would hurt the most.

"Hiya, do you have something inexpensive? Say with a screw cap?" she asked and watched him visibly shudder.

But then he eyed his displays again. "We have a box wine that might be what you're looking for? Red, white, or pink?"

That he didn't bother to say rosé said everything.

"Red, please."

"I'll be right back."

And he was, with a small brown box that claimed to have 2.5 bottles worth inside. Perfect! She thought. She could sip wine, nibble olives and watch security footage. If only Gus could see her now.

The snooty man rang up her purchase and just handed her the box, not even offering a bag. She supposed she didn't need one, but geez, he did know he was living on an island in the middle of nowhere. He wasn't on the wine board of California or anything. She got everything stowed back in the golf cart and headed home to the inn. She was anxious about what might be waiting for her.

Chapter 10

❦

Hotel guests were milling about the entrance like they should be at a boring wedding and now didn't know what to do with themselves that would be equally as unproductive. So, they stood around and chatted. Every now and then the conversational groups remixed, but they were simply reforming the same idea. Amelia was fascinated until she got bored watching with her foot on the brake. Then she honked the horn. She had never had to honk the horn on a golf cart before, so she was unprepared for it to sound like a sneezing goose. It took both her and the bystanders by surprise and her foot slipped off the brake. Luckily, she'd been headed uphill, so a crisis was easily averted.

Feeling like she had at least contributed a conversation topic, Amelia parked and headed inside. She made it back to her room unscathed. Plopping her acquisitions down on the round table in the corner, she surveyed the room. Housekeeping had been in and made the bed. They'd vacuumed up her crumbs and put new little soaps in the bathroom. If anything else had been disturbed, she couldn't tell.

She needed to go find Becky regarding the property records. She could watch the camera videos later when everyone was in bed. But remembering the unknown people that had searched her room yesterday, no way was she throwing out the delicious cheese or the as yet untried box of wine. She'd have to rig a deterrent.

She wandered around the room a few times looking at things that could be moved enough for her to get in and out but no one else. She wasn't tiny or particularly skinny however, so there wasn't much that would keep anyone out, really. Finally, inspiration hit and she dug out the new laptop and its power cable. It took another minute to get the hotel's Wi-Fi connected, but when she did, she quickly found a sound loop of a conversation. She set it to repeat endlessly and for safe measure stowed the food items in a drawer and draped a sleeve of her jacket over the edge. If it was moved when she got back… well, she'd probably drink the wine anyway. Grabbing her cell phone and her room key, she left the room and double-checked the lock. Just as she was headed down the stairs, she saw Heather out of the corner of her eye, but the former bride wasn't alone. A brawny young man of about twenty-seven was with her, his arm around her waist. Now that was interesting. Did Heather have a new boyfriend already?

When she got down to the reception desk and found Becky, she flat out asked, "Who was that with Heather?"

A blank look met her question for a few seconds and then Becky's brain appeared to connect. "Oh, that's her brother Josh."

"Has he been here all along?"

"They checked in together, so yeah, I guess. Her mom's here too. Somewhere."

"Not all in one room, I hope." That was taking family togetherness a little too far.

"No, Heather didn't want to run into Tony on the wedding day - you know, bad luck and all, so they're all staying in one of the guest cottages on the ridge."

"Hunh. I was hoping you had a few minutes to show me the property search. I'm still really unclear on how I can own anything out here, but the lawyers won't be in the office until Monday."

"Oh sure, it's super easy. I can probably even show you on your phone if you'd like."

Amelia unlocked her screen and handed the device over. Becky brought up a simple website, bookmarked it at Amelia's request and then showed her how to do a name search on the screen. "If your name was Smith, you'd have to sort through everyone, but you're the only Feelgood in here." Becky paused, her eyes widening "and you own... most of the island, according to this."

"What!"

"Well, six pages worth, anyway. See?"

Amelia saw but didn't believe. "Were they all transferred at the same time?"

"Dunno, you have to open each one and look at the history - see here's this one, that's over in Shin's Landing. I think that's Tim's place. It was transferred to you from Tony four months ago."

"What the heck?"

"You sure you and Tony weren't... you know?"

Amelia shuddered. "Absolutely not. Maybe he was trying to cover up some crime? I didn't hear anyone was after him... yet, but you never know."

Becky shrugged. "Well, you own them now. Maybe the lawyers can straighten everything out. Good luck getting rent out of Tim, though. He's a lazy good for nothing womanizer."

Confused and a bit more frightened than when she'd come down, Amelia went back up to her room. She'd been gone all of five minutes, so not surprisingly nothing had been disturbed.

She undid all her precautions, retrieved the box of wine and went in search of one of the squat glasses from the bathroom. The box had perforations where you were to take out a section, which revealed a spigot. Eying the light blue carpet and remembering the mess Tony's blood had made in the other wing, she took the whole thing into the bathroom. It looked a little weird, a cardboard box with a spigot hanging over the edge of the bathroom counter, but Amelia was past caring. She poured herself a glass and retreated to the main part of the room. She flipped through the property listings the county website now said she owned. It didn't give a lot of detail, just the street address and tax value, but there were a lot of them. She picked one at random and looked at the history. Becky had only mentioned that one had been Tony's. This one too but a month prior it had belonged to Tony's father. So clearly Tony had inherited his father's estate. That was as Amelia would have expected. Short of completely disinheriting him, his father wouldn't have had too much choice as he only had the one child. But why would Tony transfer them to her? He was about as far from a generous soul as it was possible to be so that motive was definitely out.

A soft knock came at the door. Amelia stilled and waited. It came again. "Who.... who is it?" she called out. There was no answer.

Tentatively she got up and walked over to the door. She rose up on her tiptoes to look through the peephole. Either the knocker was extremely short or they'd already left. She opened the door and looked right and left. Nothing. The hallways were empty. She shut the door again and engaged all the locks. Then she pushed the desk back in front of the door. She was going to have to sit on it and swivel her legs to get a refill on the wine (or use the bathroom). She decided she didn't care. Knowing someone couldn't just barge in was worth it.

She went back to her phone. There didn't seem to be too much else to learn from the property records but clearly, she didn't know as much about Tony as she needed to. She'd have to add research to her list of open to-do's. This murder needed to be solved and so did the mystery of how she'd just become a property magnate.

It was time to move on to the camera footage, but her glass was nearly empty. She might as well get comfortable. She gathered up her pajamas (the silky ones) and her glass. It took just a little bit of gymnastics to gyrate around so that her legs were pointing into the bathroom from the top of the desk. She landed gracefully. She changed and refilled her wine glass. The return trip was more difficult because she didn't want to spill the wine. She went ahead and retrieved the rest of her food items, deciding she might as well have an early supper. The sun was setting over the water, casting long streams of light across the sky and the gathering clouds were streaked with hot pink. There was an ominous energy in the air. She couldn't imagine leaving the room before daybreak tomorrow.

She arranged her bits of cheese, olives and bread on a couple of tissues and climbed on to the bed with her laptop. Some people might be shocked to have exactly the same thing for lunch and dinner but Amelia figured it was her favorite meal, it was completely free of murderers, and she could multitask.

So, she did. Starting with the video she'd ended when Gus has walked up behind her, the one from the inn's interior hallway. Thursday night had been a hotbed of activity. She figured out which was Tony's room when he walked out wearing a bathrobe that didn't quite close in the middle, looked both ways down the hall and then went back into the room. About an hour later, Heather went in but came out again about ten minutes later. It looked like she was crying. A few people came and went from other rooms, normal-looking people for the most part and then two women who were probably about twenty-five, but had enough makeup on to look ten years older knocked and went into Tony's room. They both wore skinny jeans and what looked like imitation leather jackets. Amelia noted the time stamp down on the little pad of paper on the nightstand. Almost exactly an hour later, the two women emerged, adjusting their clothing and rolling their eyes at each other. They wasted no time in leaving. Had that been? Were they? How had Tony found prostitutes on this remote island? Amelia realized she sounded naive even inside her own head, but still! Two nights before his wedding. What a jerk. The rest of Thursday night played without further interest so Amelia pressed the fast forward until the clock wound round to early the next morning.

Tony left, presumably to find breakfast around 8:30 am. Then the man Becky had said was Heather's brother knocked on the door. Naturally, the door didn't open and Amelia saw the man turn his body so the view of the lock was blocked. The door opened. But wait a minute, Tony wasn't there. What was he doing? Whatever it was took less than a minute because he was back out again and closing the door behind him. Then Tony came back with Heather. They were sloppily kissing, taking a few steps towards the room and then kissing some more. They went into the room and didn't come out again for two hours. They left and Tony came back by himself an hour later. Then Ralph was in the hallway clearly waiting while Sara did the housekeeping, moving up the hallway one room at a time. When she got to Tony's, he opened the door with his shirt unbuttoned. Sara took several steps back and Ralph walked into the room behind her. Tony visibly deflated and re-buttoned his shirt. Amelia paused the video and looked at the level in her wine glass. Time for a refill.

There was nothing else of interest on the hallway tape. Clearly Tony had been alive when Sara and Ralph entered his room, which the time stamp said had been 12:30. And yet all the staff had said Sara had found him dead when she'd done the room at 12:30. Something wasn't adding up. She made a note of the timestamps. At the 1:45 mark, she saw Sara without Ralph in visible distance go up to Tony's door and look carefully around before inserting her key and opening the door. The housekeeping cart wasn't in the hall and she had nothing else in her hands. Why was she going into Tony's room, when presumably he was still there? And she hadn't even knocked first. How very, very strange.

Amelia went through the rest of the tapes, but her eyes started drooping due to the lack of activity in them. The pathway one had some people coming and going. She saw Heather and her brother and then presumably her mom and a few other people come and go along the path, but none of them were carrying weapons or looking threatening, so there didn't seem to be any clues there. She shut the laptop and got up to brush her teeth. Tomorrow she'd start questioning people. The time had come to get to the bottom of this.

Chapter 11

❧

Amelia sat up wide awake. The bedside clock read 2:14 am. Thunder boomed and lightning crackled down from the sky, illuminating her room with stark shadows. Her heart thumping, she tried to lie down again but the storm was ferocious. And loud. She couldn't hear anything coming from the hallway. She got up and looked out the window. Rain was lashing against the glass and then another bolt of lightning lit up the cliff edge. Someone was out there, staring up at her room. Instinctively she took a step back and shivered. The weather had cooled considerably and her light pajamas were no longer comfortable. But she forced herself to stop shivering and look again. Whoever it was had gone. Amelia turned away and pulled the drapes closed. Then she went over and engaged the heat. Having turned on the air conditioning in Tony's room, at least she knew where it was located. Then she got back in bed with her laptop. If she was going to be awake, she might as well get in some research on Tony. Start figuring out just what was going on.

She started with social media, but after half an hour of reading Tony's pitiful and crude sexual comments to women, she gave up on that angle and started looking at public records. Ignoring all the offers to give her the complete dirt if only she'd hand over her credit card, she started digging. While Tony had grown up in Seattle, he'd left to go to school in Las Vegas which is where his mother moved when she divorced Mr. Lyle Sr. a few years later. It looked like he stayed there until his father's death. That explained a few things.

He'd also gotten married there to an Amy Hancock twenty years ago. There was no record of an Amy Hancock still living in Vegas but there were a couple of them of about the right age in California. Had she moved without him? Was one of them even her?

Amelia looked at the clock, it was now 4:30, so she might as well declare herself officially up. She got out of bed and did her swivel and kick thing to get in the bathroom. She'd brush her teeth and make coffee. But why were hotel coffee pots always so dinky? She needed serious fuel.

Bolstered with what caffeine was available she went back to the World Wide Web. It didn't have too much to offer. Tony had been a putz (not news), he had a wife, possibly ex-wife out there somewhere (which was news but not particularly informative) and that was about it. She could find nothing on the Findlater properties. They hadn't been listed for sale ever, it appeared. She looked at the clock again. Still too early for breakfast. She'd checked yesterday and nothing in the village opened for breakfast before nine on a Sunday.

Maybe this laptop had some new games. She could indulge herself for an hour with another cup of coffee and maybe gain some new perspective. Sadly, it had exactly the same games as every computer she'd used for the last ten years. Surely someone had come up with something more enduring than computer solitaire since then? And if not, why not?

Then something else caught her eye. Whoever had sold Seth this laptop hadn't bothered to remove any of their files. The documents folder was absolutely stuffed. Almost all of the files were simple dates without names She picked one at random and opened it up. It was a timed itinerary with the name T. Lyle at the top for a day about a month ago. She checked a few more, they were all for T. Lyle. She picked the one for Monday of this week. It matched with what she remembered of Tony's schedule. Amelia couldn't fathom why someone would spend that much time tracking anyone as uninteresting as Tony and if they were so stupid as to sell on the computer without taking the files off. Unless they weren't too bright. Or were the killer. Or both.

She spot-checked some of the days when she knew Tony hadn't been in the office. There were a lot of those. Actually, showing up and working wasn't his strong suit. Mostly he'd come in one or two days a week, snoop and yell at people before disappearing again. According to whoever was tracking him, a number of those 'missing' days, he'd spent on Findlater Island. And on a number of those days he'd visited 'the big house'. His time there varied from twenty minutes to just over two hours, including some late-night trips.

Amelia went looking to see what else she could find. There wasn't much but, in the pictures, she found a few group shots that included Heather and one or two that also had Tony. She was going to have to track down Seth and see what he could remember about who had sold him the computer. She needed an assistant if for nothing else but to take notes on all the things she needed to follow up on.

Shutting the laptop lid, she considered her day. Her intuition was screaming that the killer was still on the island and possibly nervous. The earliest the police would arrive was sometime tomorrow afternoon and people were still looking at her like she might have a hand in Tony's demise. She needed a sidekick. It would be nice if they could take notes, but more importantly someone to back her up if she inadvertently wandered into the killer's lair. But how? At least one and possibly all of the hotel staff had lied. She couldn't be sure if Becky knew that the other two hadn't told the whole truth so she couldn't be completely trusted. Seth was probably in the clear, but he was a bit wimpy. The other guests were all suspects and then there was Gus. Who the sheriff said was too good to have committed the murder. No, Amelia corrected herself, the sheriff had said Gus was too good to be found out, implying he had some experience with killing people. Definitely not Gus. Maybe Seth's slightly beanstalk physique was still better than nothing. She'd try and find him after breakfast and ask. Maybe Becky knew where he hung out when he wasn't at work.

But she didn't have to hunt him down because when she was dressed and ready to go into town, she found him at the bottom of the stairs in the hallway outside reception. "Oh hi, um Ms...? I was just on my way up to find you."

"Oh?" Who the heck had given out her room number to a total stranger?

"That computer I sold you? The guy wants it back. Said he'd made a mistake and didn't want to get rid of it."

"Tough. I bought it fair and square."

"I know. That's what I told him. That's why everyone has to sign a consent form before I purchase. But he offered me $500 to get it back. I'm willing to split it with you."

So, this mystery seller had originally sold it for $50 and then wanted it back for $500. He must really have seller's regret. "Who sold it to you, again?"

"Oh, I can't say. Just like I didn't give him your name. I just told him I'd come and ask."

"Hunh. And who was it who told you I was staying here or apparently my room number?"

"Oh, Becky's my sister. Almost all the tourists stay in three places and I have relatives that work at all of them, so that wasn't hard."

Darn it, clearly Seth had the makings of a great sidekick. But being Becky's brother when Becky was not in the clear put a definite shadow on things. "I see. Well, it's not for sale until I can get off the island and back to my own. You'll just have to tell your customer no."

Seth looked a little nervous. "Um, okay. A deal's a deal."

"Is this guy large?"

His Adam's apple bobbed convulsively. "Yeah."

"And blond?"

"I guess so."

Amelia's mind immediately went to Heather's brother. "Well, I'd keep a low profile if I were you. I'm going to." And she turned and retraced her steps. She was not leaving that laptop unattended in her room. She'd have to risk taking it with her or find someplace else to stash it temporarily. She ran back up the stairs, retrieved the laptop and her large shoulder bag and came back down again. Seth was nowhere to be seen.

Outside it was raining, not a huge surprise after the storm last night, but a big change from the previously beautiful weather. The golf cart was not set up for all weather, so by the time she parked near the pub she was wet through.

An equally wet dog was waiting just outside the entrance. He didn't seem to be tied up to anything and his fur was long and in various shades of wet gray. His big brown eyes looked at Amelia hopefully, but he didn't approach. "Nice dog," she said, hoping that would keep him from putting muddy paws on her pants. Maybe it worked. In any event, he sat there like a library statue. Amelia went in and tried to slide most of the rain off her face.

The pub was packed. She had to wait for a table, so while she stood there, slightly steaming from the warmth of bodies around her, she surveyed the crowd. Heather and presumably her brother and mother were seated at a four-top by the far wall. She didn't see anyone else she knew. When a table opened up, she was delighted to see it was right next to Heather. Seeing as how she was pretty sure Heather's brother might have been the original owner of the laptop, she absolutely did not want to get it out, so she took out her bullet journal instead. She needed to catch up on her journaling and take some notes for this case. Might as well do it over breakfast.

Amelia pretty much already had the menu memorized so she started making an immediate to-list for the day while she waited on a waitress. One swung by with a "coffee?" which Amelia responded to by holding out an empty cup. Then she went back to her list. She needed some clothes and some shoes. Then she needed to pick up some groceries that would keep in her room, just in case she couldn't come in to town for every meal. The waitress finally came by with a pad. Amelia ordered the Western omelet with hash browns and sourdough toast. Maybe if she ate a big breakfast, she could skip lunch and get a lot done before dinner.

She made a new list in her hot pink journal for all the people she needed to talk to in order to figure out why she owned half the island (or more) and who had killed Tony. She was increasingly of the opinion that whoever had done so had done the world a favor. She looked up with a smile when the waitress plopped a loaded platter down in front of her.

"You! How dare you come in and sit next to me?! Murderer!" The dramatic accusation that sent the entire pub into an excited hush had come from Heather.

Amelia looked over at her calmly. "I haven't killed anyone. I have no reason to. What about you? Did you sign a prenup that's now taken effect?" Low-level chatter erupted at that from the other tables. Everyone was watching and those with their backs to the two women had turned around. Only the servers were up and about delivering food. All of which was ignored as people took in the show.

Heather's response was to burst into tears. Again. But this time her brother, or at least who Amelia suspected was her brother, interjected hotly. "Heather wouldn't hurt a fly. But Tony hurt her, and so did you! You should be nicer to people."

"Who are you exactly?"

"I'm Josh."

"Well Josh, maybe you could explain how I could have hurt Heather when I only met her on Friday?"

"You didn't have to meet her. You refused to give Tony a divorce for two long years. And now you've stolen all the property that should have been hers."

"Um, Josh? Who do you think I am?"

He gave her a dirty condescending look, "You're Tony's wife. Ex-wife...whatever."

Amelia found her stomach rebelling slightly at even the thought of being married to someone like Tony. "No, not now, not ever. I worked for Tony after his father died. That's it and frankly, that was too much."

Murmuring started around the room. Amelia rolled her eyes that anyone would see that as a confession.

Heather finally found her voice again. "You're lying. Tony said you had the property and that's why we couldn't stay in the mansion because he didn't own it anymore."

"What mansion?"

"The big old one on the hill. He said his ex wanted all his property and he didn't know what else to do."

Amelia pondered that. "What's his ex's name?"

"Amy something."

"Well my name's not Amy anything. It's Amelia Feelgood."

Josh snickered when she got to 'Feelgood'. His mother frowned at him, but she had yet to say a word. "You're lying."

"Nope." Amelia dug out her driver's license and showed to Heather without letting go of the edges.

"It could be a fake."

"Why? Are you sure you didn't benefit from Tony's death?"

Heather harrumphed and got up to leave. Her brother and mother went scurrying behind her to pay the check and get their coats on. Amelia turned back to her breakfast that she had yet to taste. It was delicious. The ham was lovely and home cut, not salvaged from deli cold cuts. She poured ketchup on top of the hash browns and dug in.

The rest of the diners turned back to their meals, but not their conversations. Ears were clearly straining to catch any new developments. Amelia made room on the corner of the small table for her journal and jotted down the names and other details that had been unconsciously divulged. Josh had been built. He spent serious time in the gym but his intelligence made Heather look like a whiz kid. Had they always had that dynamic or had he had a traumatic brain injury or something?

When she was done, Amelia got up to pay the check. More people were waiting for tables so not lingering seemed the fair thing to do. As she was paying, she asked the woman at the register, "Can you tell me where I can find some extra clothes until the ferry is back? Maybe not too expensive?"

The woman looked thoughtful for a minute as she rang up the check. "Well, there's the touristy place across the way where you can buy Findlater t-shirts and the like, but if I were you, I'd head to the thrift store."

"Oh! You have a thrift store? Where is it?"

"It's in a converted house right behind the church. You can't miss it. It's only open on the weekends."

"Perfect! thank you." Amelia was delighted. She didn't typically buy clothes there, but she loved poking around junk shops and thrift stores looking for hidden little bijoux treasures. It felt so very eclectically French somehow. Or at least it was in her mind. She exited the pub with more of a bounce in her step than she'd had for a few days. It died abruptly when she saw who was sitting in her golf cart. The gray dog she'd seen earlier was happily stretched out on the bench seat. He looked up at her but didn't raise his head. His tail thumped slightly. "Oh dear. Out! Out, doggie, out!" she waved it towards the side but the dog just seemed to sink further into the seat. Amelia looked at it closer, He had a red leather collar on so she tentatively reached out and tugged on it slightly. The dog didn't move but gave her a sad, reproachful look. "Gaah!" Amelia vented in frustration. She turned around and marched back into the pub. The woman at the register looked up in surprise. "There's a gray dog in my vehicle. Do you know who it belongs to?"

"Shaggy, with a red collar?"

Amelia nodded.

"Oh, that's Sadie. She's friendly."

"But I need to leave."

"She goes with whom she likes. Her owner died last year so she's been pretty much adopted by the island. She goes where she likes and whoever has her feeds her until she moves on. She takes herself to the vet once a month for a bath and they check her over when she visits so she's clean."

"She takes herself to the vet?"

"Yup, darnedest thing."

"And she's a she?"

"That too."

Amelia shook her head in bewilderment and went back to the golf cart. Sadie hadn't moved a muscle.

"Okaaaay, I'm sorry I thought you were a boy dog." Sadie raised her head and tilted it inquiringly.

"But I need to get going with my errands so if you're coming you have to move over."

Amelia inched her hip onto the seat and sort of crowded Sadie into a sitting position. She didn't seem to mind though, and when Amelia turned the key and backed up the golf cart, Sadie let her tongue hang out.

"Right," Amelia said in the same tone of voice that a Victorian army officer might have uttered 'Charge!' and headed for the church and the lure of the thrift store behind it.

A small crowd of worshipers were gathered under black umbrellas in front of the church. Amelia couldn't see why. Surely the doors were open? But she didn't dare venture any closer for fear of being guilted into attending services. Her mother never lost an opportunity to remind her that her soul was on a knife edge, which is why they only talked a few times a year. She averted her gaze and kept the cart trundling along the road until she could turn a corner. There was also a small crowd in front of the thrift store. Just as Amelia pulled into a parking space the doors opened and people rushed in. One late arrival looked over, "Hi, Sadie!"

Sadie barked but did not get out of the cart. Amelia looked at her in disbelief. Why would this dog want to go with a perfect stranger when she clearly had friends? Maybe she'd move on while Amelia took her time in the thrift store.

It wasn't big, but it did have a lot of clothes. She poked through the racks and found a few things that would do for a few days and some newer shoes that looked just broken in enough to avoid blisters. Amelia wasn't crazy about wearing shoes someone else had worn but she found new thick socks and well, needs must. To reward herself for so much practical thinking, she took a tour through the small housewares section. She found a beautiful wine glass that looked like it was hand blown for only a dollar. It was going back to her room. As she was passing the book section, rather quickly because she didn't need anything to read, a title jumped out at her, The History of Findlater Island. It had been written about twenty years prior, but it had pictures and blessedly an even more detailed map than the tourist board's. It even showed a dot in the middle that said Original Findlater Mansion. Was that what Heather had been referring to?

Since her hands were now completely full, Amelia took that as a sign to leave and made her way to the register. All of her purchases came to nine dollars and seventy-five cents, with tax. Satisfied she went back to the golf cart. Sadie was still in position. Amelia shrugged and stored her purchases in the footwell. She still had her wine box in her room; she wasn't that much of a lush but she did need some food. And apparently, she was now responsible for feeding Sadie as well. She drove the golf cart down to the little grocery store that served the island. Most everyone did stocking up trips on the mainland, but this filled in the gaps. It was not a pretentious establishment but they kept some fancy stuff by the door for tourists. The rainy day had put ozone in the air and Amelia paused to breathe it in. There was a freshness to breathing in spring rain that was unlike any other.

Inside, she did a quick tour around the aisles and discovered everything by the door was twice the price of similar items on the shelves. Since she didn't have a refrigerator, she was somewhat limited in what she could get, but she assembled an assortment of cookies, crackers, and hard cheese. The olives took a lot of thinking. She could buy plain black ones or pay the doorway premium for the mixed ones in olive oil. She went for the mixed. She decided she needed the brain food. A man who clearly worked there because of his red apron was restocking the fresh pizzas in the cooler. "Excuse me."

He looked up and smiled "yes?"

"Do you know Sadie, the dog?"

"Of course, everyone knows Sadie."

"Well she's decided I'm her next place of call. I heard I'm supposed to feed her but I don't know what she eats."

"Oh wow, I've not heard of her taking to a tourist before. This way."

He led her down an aisle that started with mustard, ended in toilet paper and had pet food about midway on the left. "She's partial to this brand, either the mixed seafood grill or the beef."

"And how much do I feed her?"

"One can a day. She'll either eat it in one meal or if you're going to be home, she's happy to have it split into breakfast or dinner. Oh, and she likes these treats." He pointed to an almost local brand that used pretty cookie cutters to make cute designs.

"How long is she likely to stay with me?"

"Don't know. Like I said she's usually with locals. That can be from a couple of days to a couple of months."

"Right. Well I definitely won't be here that long." Amelia decided to get three cans and the treats. If Sadie decided to stay longer than she could come back. She'd have eaten the human cookies herself by then and probably need a refill.

Pondering her new friend as she drove back up the hill to the inn, Amelia decided Sadie might not be such a bad thing. She'd never had a pet and while she quite wanted the companionship, she'd always felt that she couldn't have one until she got to France as she wouldn't want to leave a cat or dog behind. Sadie clearly belonged on Findlater

Island, so Amelia could learn a little about having a dog without actually having one. She suspected she might be more of a cat person, anyway.

Chapter 12

❦

Back at the inn once again, Amelia parked the golf cart in the corral and headed inside. She half expected Sadie to just hang out there since that's what she'd done at the stores but no. As soon as Amelia pulled open the front door, Sadie zipped in, through reception and headed for the stairs.

"How does she know?"

"Who?" Becky asked as she came in from the back room.

"Oh um." Amelia was pretty sure she'd seen a no pets policy. Then she remembered that for the moment at least, she owned the darned place. When that changed, she'd have already left the island. "Do you know Sadie? She came back with me."

"Really? I've never heard of her hanging out with anyone but locals. Well, tell her she's welcome to hang out with me if you're not around."

"Um, will do?" Baffled at the dog's behavior and how everyone seemed to think it was normal, Amelia headed back to her room to regroup.

Sadie was patiently waiting in front of her door. "How did you know it was this room, Sadie?"

"She probably followed your scent," Ralph said as he came down the hall with the housekeeping cart.

"Oh, that actually makes sense." And a correlating idea popped into Amelia's head. Maybe Sadie could sniff out the killer too.

"Hiya Sadie!" Ralph leaned down to scratch the dog behind the ears. Sadie took it as her due but got up and ducked into the room as soon as Amelia unlocked it. She jumped up on the bed and barked happily.

"Shhhh. You're the only dog allowed here. Don't make trouble." Sadie rolled over on her back and folded over all four paws, tucking her head back so that only her little tiny front teeth showed. Amelia giggled and set her bags down on the table. She took out her new wine glass and took it into the bathroom to wash it. Then she set it on top of the TV until she could enjoy using it in the evening. She took the thrift store clothes out and sniffed them. They were a bit musty. She needed to ask Becky if there was a way to do laundry. There had to be as they did all the sheets and towels on site.

Putting the History of Findlater Island on the table with her laptop, she got down to investigating. Now that she had the right name of Tony's ex, they were easy to find as a couple. It took a little digging through court records to find the actual date. The divorce had become final the day Tony died. And yet he was getting married the next day. How had he gotten a wedding license to marry Heather? Surely that was cutting it a little fine. The ex was now living in Seattle. Small world. Amelia studied the tiny social media profile picture she'd found. She didn't think she'd ever seen this woman before but… it might not be a recent picture.

Josh wasn't at all hard to track down. He and Heather were clearly tight and discretion was not his middle name. His profile page was wide open and he openly discussed all the steroids he was using to try to 'bulk up'. The world was discriminating against him and his sister because they were 'beautiful people'. The world was apparently full of haters. And top of his hit list was the woman who owned the property that rightly belonged to his sister. They had plans you see, to create a body building and yoga retreat until this nasty woman had ruined everything.

Amelia frowned in concentration. So, they hadn't known that Tony was the one to transfer the property. There went that motive.

Had Heather killed him in a fit of rage? Amelia doubted it. Rage brought on wrinkles and Heather did seem genuinely distraught that she didn't get to walk down the aisle. It might be more about the attention than Tony, but she could have murdered him after the ceremony and gained quite a bit more. Heather seemed savvy enough to know that much, at least. Josh, she wasn't so sure about. Maybe she'd missed something incriminating on the laptop.

She pulled it back towards her and did another file search. Nothing she hadn't already opened. But hey... maybe... she pulled up the browser and looked in the history. His email account was on the top. Had he been silly enough to leave the login information? She clicked the tab. Why yes, he had. She was in BaywatchJosh's email. But seriously, that address? Was he for real?

He seemed to think so anyway. His email was full of suggestive flirting with women who could have been his female clones. Every week or so he emailed Tony asking for money. He always couched it as something Heather wanted or how it would benefit Heather, but it was clearly a request for a cash handout. At first Tony replied with a 'No." Then it got ruder and then he stopped responding. The last request from Josh was earlier in the week. You could say one thing for him, he didn't give up.

Rather than go downstairs, Amelia picked up the room phone to call Becky about the laundry. It turned out there were guest services she could use and she didn't even have to go downstairs. It was right at the end of the hall by the ice machine. She bundled up her new and old clothes and headed down the hall. Sadie remained in her upside-down position so Amelia took that as a sign that she didn't want to come along. She set two loads going with the complimentary detergent and headed back. Her footsteps slowed though when she heard a couple arguing in a room just a few doors down from the service room.

"You need to get a lawyer, Amy. He owed you. It's all rightfully yours."

"I don't want it, Anthony, so what does it matter. You haven't done something stupid, have you? Tell me you didn't."

"What are you talking about? I haven't done anything."

"You're sure?"

"What could I have done? I've been with you holding your hand all weekend."

"Yeah. But, not all weekend. What about Saturday night?"

"You mean after he was killed."

Oh my God. They were talking about Tony! And that woman was asking the guy if he'd had something to do with it. Amelia leaned in closer to the door and then realized what she was doing. She quickly made a note of the room number and then skedaddled back to her room. She wrote it down in her notebook and then called Becky again.

"Hey Becky, who's in room 212?"

"Umm. Let me check. Amy Henderson. Why?"

"Oh, I was passing from the laundry and I thought I recognized her voice from like high school. But I didn't know any Amy Henderson. Thanks."

"Sure."

Amelia turned to Sadie who'd righted herself and curled into a ball. "There's no such thing as coincidences."

Chapter 13

✑

"Sadie, I'm going on reconnaissance. You can't stay here by yourself." Amelia informed the dog as authoritatively as she could muster. Sadie leaped up with a canine grin and jumped off the bed, arriving at the room door with only one touchdown in between. Then she sat there and whined as though she'd been waiting patiently for an hour.

Amelia rolled her eyes and wondered if Sadie was willing to come along with her. She didn't have a leash, but walking the dog would be a good cover for going down the wooded trail to the guest cottages. That was her intended destination despite a few misgivings about going by herself. She walked down the stairs with Sadie by her heels. Reception was empty.

The weather had resolved itself to a slightly damp mist, an iconic weather variation of the Pacific Northwest. Amelia was of two minds on it: it tended to make her hair curl, far more so than outright rain, but on the other hand, it was a perfect toning facial. At the edge of the clearing surrounding the inn, she paused briefly to look back at the mansion. It was hard to believe it had ever been a single-family residence. It seemed almost foreboding from this angle, perched on the edge of a cliff. She searched for and found Tony's room and then looked to see if she could find the hidden service door. It wasn't visible from this vantage point at all. Then she noticed something strange. There was a trellis attached to the wall on the lower level, but whatever was meant to be growing on it had been cut to the ground.

She wandered closer to get a good look.

Grabbing onto the trellis, she tested it for weight. It was very solid. Certainly, someone of her size could have climbed it, but did it go all the way up? She craned her neck to see. It went far enough up that a strong person could have hoisted themselves up on to the ledge. She was not going to be testing that theory. Particularly since it didn't matter all that much as it would have been possible for the killer to either have entered his room the normal way through the door or come from the patio side from the service entrance. Sadie gave a quiet woof, still waiting by the edge of the clearing.

Amelia scanned the ground for any clues. Nothing stood out. There were a few cigarette butts and some candy wrappers, but they were thoroughly mixed in with the dead leaves and looked like they'd been there for several months. Probably from when they cleared off the patio in the autumn. She turned back towards the trail and the dog. "Ready, Sadie?"

They walked down a narrow dirt trail that meandered around the trunks of giant evergreens. The boughs overhead kept even the fine mist out so the ground was dry, covered in old fir needles with a small fern here and there. It smelled damp and ferny, with Christmassy evergreen notes. Small wildflowers were just coming into bloom on the forest floor. Occasionally Sadie scampered off for a minute, chasing squirrels or ghosts, but she quickly came back and resumed her spot in front of Amelia. Around a half mile in, the trees thinned and then stopped. A wide semicircle of green grass hosted five cottages sprinkled randomly around. There was a small pond in the middle and the ocean to the left. What was a sheer cliff at the inn had dwindled to a protective ledge of about five feet, dropping down to a sand and pebble beach. There was a maze of driftwood decorating the edges of the beach. "How lovely," Amelia said to Sadie. "Why aren't we staying here?"

Sadie rushed to the beach, using a small boat ramp hidden in one corner to get down to it. Amelia slowly walked towards the access point, listening and looking for anything out of place. Everything seemed deserted but there were cars pulled up to each of the cottages. It would be a bit of a pain to walk through the woods to get a golf cart to go get breakfast, she supposed. Still, these places must have kitchens. And clearly, there must be a road somewhere. She moseyed, deliberately slowing her steps as she followed the well-worn path between the cottages and towards the beach. Nothing seemed out of place when she joined Sadie on the sand. Sadie had found a stick. A very big stick, about four feet long. She had to keep putting it down and readjusting her grip because it kept going out of balance and one end would drag on the ground. Amelia found a thick log to sit on that was up against the embankment and watched Sadie play.

It was then that she heard voices approaching overhead. "Where did that dog come from?" said a woman's voice suspiciously.

"I think it's a stray, I saw it wandering around town by itself. I wouldn't worry about it," a man responded.

"Still, way out here? Anybody there?" she called out loudly.

Amelia held her breath. Sadie thankfully acted as if nothing was out of the ordinary.

"When can we get out of here?"

"I told you, the ferry won't be back in until the police have come."

"Couldn't we hire a boat? You know it's not a good idea to cut things so fine."

"We don't have much choice; we'd have to leave the car and it leads right back to us. Well you, anyway. Unless you're prepared to join your friends in Mexico?

"Hardly," the woman said dryly. "The whole point was to get away from that lifestyle. Paris, baby. That's what I'm holding out for."

No! Amelia shouted silently. They sounded like criminals and they wanted to move to France too! They couldn't corrupt her dreams like that.

"They're only coming to look at a murder. Not traipsing around through the woods. Besides, I hear the fiancée is telling everyone in town his assistant did it. That'll keep 'em busy for a few days. Heck if they're green, they'll probably just haul her away and not look further."

The woman laughed. "That sounds about right. Okay, let's go show our face in town, make like good little tourists."

Amelia tilted her head up. All she could see of the couple was a man's hand with a bit of dark tattoo showing below the wrist and a navy jacket sleeve. This was the guy she'd seen on the surveillance tape.

"At least now we don't have to send a ho to his room every time there's a drop when he's on the island."

"Don't you think he figured it out?"

"Tony wasn't what you'd call a deep thinker."

Amelia listened to their voices fade as they walked away. Her heart was pounding. Was it true that Heather's rumor was spreading around town? She'd certainly told a few people right in front of her so it probably was. Amelia was not going to be arrested though. She rethought that. Well, not as long as she solved it first. And what would be her motive anyway? She thought back to all the abuse she'd suffered in the office. All right, she had a motive. Time to get busy since she knew she hadn't done it. Sadie came up and plopped down beside her, breathing heavily. She'd worn herself out digging holes in the sand.

Amelia checked her phone and made herself wait twenty minutes before getting up from her hidden spot. They would be taking the road out, so she and Sadie had better return via the woods. Time to get serious about this investigation.

The walk back went a little slower because Sadie was clearly worn out. Amelia took her back to her room and opened the can of dog food, only then realizing that she didn't have any kind of a dish to put it in. She confiscated the tray that went under the coffee maker in the bathroom and decided that would do. Sadie seemed pleased and practically inhaled it all. Amelia left her to it and went down the hall to move her laundry into the dryer. Then she headed downstairs on a mission. First task was to find Becky.

It was easily accomplished as Becky was sitting at the computer in the back office playing solitaire.

"Becky, can you get me a list of everyone staying here on Friday, Saturday and today, including the guest cottages?"

"Yeah, since you're the owner and all. Do you want a printout?"

"That would be great. Oh, and where does the road to the cottages go or start from?"

"Not much of anywhere really. It goes past the old big house and then circles around some small places and connects up to Shin's Landing."

"Right, who lives in the old house?"

"Nobody. It's been empty for years. It's too far away from town and it doesn't have a water view. Miserable place to heat, and it's ready to fall down."

"Who owns it?"

Becky looked at her a little funny. "Tony. It's the one property on the island listed under his name."

"Oh! So, then nobody will mind if I go check it out?"

"Suit yourself, but be careful, the floorboards might be rotted. Not that I'd know of course," she said, hurriedly pulling a few sheets of paper out of the printer and handing them to Amelia. "There you go, that's the guest list."

"Great! Thanks."

Amelia retreated upstairs. She needed to go check out that house. But first, she was going to look over the list.

It didn't have all the guests' names on it, just who had checked in and the number of people in their party. But she could narrow down the cottages since she knew Heather, and two of them were rented by a couple with multiple children. Her villains did not seem to be the sort to drag kids along, nor had they mentioned them That left a Mr. Simon Woodrow and a Cassie Mayhew. She checked both of them online. They were innocuous and there were so many people with those names that it was impossible to know who was standing on that bank.

She thought about what to do next while she retrieved her clean laundry and brought it back to the room. She folded and put away most of it, but left out one of her thrift store outfits. Nobody had seen her in these and they were dark colors that would blend into the surroundings. Absolutely no flair about them at all. But sometimes you had to sacrifice for the greater good.

She got dressed and looked in the mirror. It was awful. She put on the comfortable shoes and then wondered how to disguise her hair or if she needed to. But it did look very at odds with her new grungy outfit. She would stop in town on her way to this mysterious mansion and buy a hat or a headband or something.

Resolved, she woke Sadie up from her nap and they headed down to get a golf cart. She had to leave Sadie there and go back to her room because she forgot the book with the map. Once retrieved, she headed back down again, passing Sara and Ralph having a furiously whispered conversation in the corner of reception. Ralph had his arm over Sara's head against the wall and he was leaning into her, imposing. Sara wasn't taking it quietly. Her shoulders were braced and she was giving as good as she got, only occasionally forgetting to keep her voice to near silent.

"Everything okay?" Amelia asked.

They broke apart as if a firecracker had gone off in the room. "Teenagers!" Ralph said and turned to leave.

Sara responded with "Old farts!" and shoved a candy wrapper into the pocket of her uniform and went the other way. Neither of them looked at Amelia.

"Well, that was weird," Amelia said to an empty room.

❧

Sadie was waiting for her in the golf cart so they tootled their way into the village, stopping briefly at the tourist shop, housed in yet another medieval building, to buy a navy baseball cap that said Findlater Island in gold embroidery. It was hideous and exactly what she was looking for. She paid and plopped it on her head immediately. It made her completely anonymous, just another tourist rambling around the little island.

Back in the golf cart, she checked the map again to see which road led out to the service village. In the end, she realized that most of them did, or rather everything circled back into town unless you kept turning northwest and then you found yourself on the one road that led out. Since the golf cart maxed out at twenty miles per hour, it took them about half an hour to get there but the ride was pleasant and only a few cars passed them. Amelia was curious to see Shin's Landing after hearing so much about it, but while quaint, it turned out to not be very remarkable. All of the buildings were basic squares and rectangles. A few had a dormer window on the second floor and they were all in various stages of repair, but that was about it. It was clearly not part of the original fantasy, but was practical in every detail. The fact that there was a small harbor with docks and fishing boats all smelling of fish clearly marked the demarcation between the tourist zone and the locals.

It wasn't difficult to find the road that continued through and into the woods. It got dark under the trees quickly and the road was so little used that moss was growing on the pavement. A few deer stared out from the salal bushes and there was a decidedly eerie undertone. Some driveways marked private led off from the road but wherever they led to was far enough back to not be visible from the road. Only one had anything distinguishing and it was an elaborately carved signed that said 'This way to the 3 bears' house.' It was framed by at least twelve red and white signs that said private or no trespassing and violators will be prosecuted with one beware of the dog.

"Wow, someone really doesn't want company," Amelia remarked to Sadie, who was looking down the lane. Her tail was wagging enthusiastically but no way was Amelia going down there. She did pause to check her map though and saw a 3 bears notation just below the turn to the big house. Maybe the book would tell her about that place later. They headed farther down the road until they hit an unmarked turn. This must be it. Amelia turned the golf cart into the rut and slowed down. The bushes were untended but there were signs that at least a few vehicles passed this way occasionally. She pulled up to a circular drive in front of what once had been a very grand mansion indeed. Broken Edwardian glasshouses were arranged in a long row by a crumbling walled garden. The house itself was wildly Victorian with no less than four turrets, one at each corner and elaborate brickwork framing all the edges. There were at least three big holes in the roof. An arched porch led to a massive carved oak door that stood slightly ajar.

Amelia and Sadie looked at each other. Amelia shrugged and they both got out of the golf cart. Amelia fished a small LED flashlight out of her bag and turned it on. Pulling the door open a little more, she slipped through and into what truly felt like a haunted house. There wasn't much left to it. All the furnishings had been removed, even the light fixtures. Water had run down the wallpaper and it all smelled mildewy. It was very dark. In the entry, it looked like it had once been green on green flocked velvet wallpaper. Oak wainscoting dressed out the room. Amelia could see what Becky meant about the floors - there were sections that looked like they had splintered and were about ready to go. If she fell through, would anyone think to come looking here? Some crushed beer cans in the corner caught her eye. Yeah, maybe they would. This looked like maybe it was a favorite teenage hangout spot, which might explain a few things. Keeping to the edges of the room, Amelia headed towards the right-hand door and peeked into the next room. This must have been a parlor. A beautiful tiled fireplace in cobalt blue stood out in the gloom, but it was the only remnant of its former glory. She kept going. The rooms were arranged in a loose circle around the central hallway. At the back was a kitchen. Bright spots of color caught Amelia's eye beneath the old cast iron range. She leaned in closer. Candy - Skittles if she wasn't mistaken. Definitely teenagers. At least the old stove was still here and hadn't been ripped out. She opened the oven door to look inside. Empty except for some strange white powder. Cleanser, maybe? But who would be cleaning a stove in an empty house?

She straightened up and looked around for Sadie. She wasn't there. "Sadie?" she called softly, somehow not wanting to make a lot of noise. Nothing.

Amelia continued around the circle wandering through a library with empty shelves except for a recently dead pigeon. Yuck. And then she was at the foot of the grand staircase that led upstairs. She had one foot on the first step when she heard footsteps coming from the front door. She looked around for a place to hide, but the only actual door was on the small space built under the stairs. She stuffed herself inside and had to hold the latch as there wasn't quite enough room to shut the door. The footsteps paused.

"Ms. Feelgood? Amelia? Are you here?" a man called out.

Heck, who was that? She'd heard the voice before. It wasn't the guy from the beach. She needed a closer look. She pushed the little door out just a tiny bit and tried to crane her head around the corner. Unfortunately, she lost her balance and tumbled to the floor with an ooof!

"Ah, Ms. Feelgood, I presume," the man said with a laugh. Amelia looked up. It was Gus. At least that question was answered, but did she like the answer? She really wasn't sure.

"What are you doing here?"

"Finding out what you're doing here. This isn't a safe place to explore." He handed her the cap that had fallen off her head when she fell.

"Well, apparently Tony owned it. I overheard someone say something about a shipment."

"Oh yes?" The smile faded quickly from his face, his eyes going cold and sharp. "What do you know about it?"

"N-n-n-othing," she stuttered.

"Then you shouldn't stick your nose in places where it could get cut off. Even small islands have criminals."

Amelia shivered. "Are you one of them?" It wasn't like she expected an honest answer, but she asked just to see how he would react. He clearly had an ample supply of self-control. What would it take to make that slip?

"I'm retired," he said easily with a half-smile.

"Sadie seems to like you." Amelia eyed the dog that instead of helping her was clearly infatuated with the man, leaning against his leg and leaning her chin up to be scratched.

"Sadie is, well... who knows how she thinks. She likes beef bourguignon. But hell, who doesn't?" He scratched Sadie's gray chin gently.

"You didn't say why you're here."

"I did. I came looking for you, you passed my place on the way in. I was out running when you drove your little cart down the lane."

"Do you live at the three bears place?"

"Yes."

"Why do you have a giant sign and then all those no trespassing signs?"

His jaw clenched. "I'm required by law to keep the giant sign. I tried taking it down and the local busybody committee took me to court. But they can't stop me from adding more signs."

"Oh, I see." She didn't but clearly it was a touchy subject. "I don't own your house too, do I?"

"No. Otherwise, they'd have taken you to court."

They stood there facing each other. "Don't you know what you own?" he inquired cautiously.

"Not really. Like I told you on Friday, I just found out and it's about six pages on the county website."

His eyes widened almost imperceptibly. "And you didn't buy any of it."

"No. I've never been here before this weekend."

"Have you seen enough to satisfy your curiosity?"

"For now." She sighed, giving in. He waited for her to lead the way out, probably so he'd know she was really leaving she thought snidely. His concern was nice if it was really concern, concerning if it was anything more suspicious.

She got back in the golf cart and Sadie jumped up on the seat beside her.

"Why do you live all the way out here?"

"I like my privacy."

"I see." He waited while she circled the driveway and then drove out. In the rear-view mirror, she saw him jogging behind her, presumably headed back to his place.

Chapter 14

❦

As she drove back to town as fast as the golf cart would allow, Amelia couldn't quite shake the feeling that she was being watched. The cart bumped over the old pavement as she pushed it to the maximum. She glanced over at Sadie, but the dog seemed unconcerned. She was panting slightly, sitting up on the seat and sticking her nose into the wind. "Well, Sadie? Should we go back and have dinner in the room? Or stop in town?"

Sadie looked at her and thwapped her feathery tail on the seat. "Right, my call, hunh?" Suddenly Amelia was exhausted. All the stress and excitement of the last few days hit her across her shoulders. "Room it is, then. We'll eat and watch some silly TV." Sadie settled down on the seat with a groan, laying her head between her paws.

It took a while to drive through the village. The tourists were starting to look a little bored. Like they'd already checked out all the little shops and didn't have anything else to do. So, they were mostly standing around in small clusters that spilled into the street. The pub looked like it was hopping but that was the extent of the excitement. She had to wait for the people standing in the street to get out of the way. One of them was Heather, who glared at her. Amelia couldn't help but wonder what Tony had told Heather about her. She'd probably never know now, and maybe that was for the best. Otherwise, she might have been the one to kill him.

A group of teenagers swarmed around the corner. Gangly young men, trying to act like girls weren't the only thing on their minds, swaggered with long thin arms flung around the shoulders of said girls. One of them looked like Sara, the girl who had found Tony in his room, but Amelia couldn't be sure. She was wearing tight ripped jeans and gothy black eye makeup along with a matching scowl. The boy attached to her like a limpet was digging his fingers into her shoulder. Amelia didn't like the looks of that. She slowed the golf cart to a crawl next to the group. Giving the offending young man the forceful frown of an unimpressed middle-aged woman, she called to the girl, "Sara, is that you?"

"Who wants to know?" the young man answered in her place.

"Her employer," Amelia answered dryly. "Sara, everything okay here? Can I give you a lift home?"

"I'm fine," the girl spit out, shaking off the arm of the punk kid and moving up to join two of the other girls.

Amelia continued on to the inn, distracted by what she'd just seen. The island seemed so idyllic. It was hard to imagine anyone being disgruntled unless the tourist store was sold out of embroidered baseball caps. She tried to imagine life on the island as a teenager and fell flat. Amelia had spent her teenage years doing everything possible to not be a labeled product of her environment. She'd worn clothes thirty years too old for her and walked around with poetry books she never took the time to read. Maybe Sara was doing basically the same thing.

Back in the room, she offered Sadie some of the dog biscuits the store clerk had recommended. Sadie graciously accepted, taking the biscuits up on the bed to gnaw in peace. Amelia fixed herself a little of this and a little of that from her stores in the bureau drawers and poured a glass of wine from the box still balanced on the edge of the bathroom counter. She put it all on the small table with the computer and went looking for the TV remote. Eventually, she located it in the drawer of the nightstand and turned the TV on. Being so far from the mainland, the only options were the twenty or so channels offered by the nearest cable company and it was clear it was a budget package. It was still early in the evening, so everything was local news and reruns of things she'd seen. A few old westerns didn't hold her interest. PBS was midway through a special on drug running. She paused there when the voiceover said 'rural islands near the Canadian border make the perfect drop off point' with the same tone of mild interest as if saying that 'rural islands are the perfect breeding ground for blue-footed boobies.' A shiver ran down her spine. She was on a rural island near the Canadian border. But surely the Coast Guard kept an eye on these things. Heck, if PBS knew about it, surely they did?

She set down the remote control and started eating, waiting for the show to reassure her that all was well. But instead, it followed a handoff of cocaine and heroin from California through to upper Canada. Thankfully the island they were showing wasn't Findlater, but it didn't look all that different, well minus the medieval re-creations. It was a little island with a few clusters of houses and some folks that felt cheated by the system and happy to add to their income with a little light drug running. Amelia watched the package being handed off between fishing boats in the open water with interest.

Sipping her wine, Amelia contemplated the sad state of the world. She really needed a relaxing hobby, like knitting or something. Except when she'd tried it that one time, she'd nearly stabbed the woman trying to instruct her in the eye. Twice. With renewed conviction, she cleared away the remnants of her dinner, poured some more wine, and dug out her journal and the book she'd purchased. It was time to think about something besides murder and drugs. With a deeply contented sigh, Sadie seemed to agree as she nestled her wedge-shaped head between her front paws.

Amelia started paging through the book on hobbies, eliminating the things she'd already tried: knitting and whittling. Her history said hobbies involving sharp implements should probably be avoided. But cheese making sounded interesting. So did winemaking. Both were French pursuits, weren't they? So, they might help her make friends when she relocated to Europe. But then stained glass had a colorful appeal, or quilt making. She could picture herself curled up in front of a fire with a nice cat and sewing calmly. She'd never really thought of gardening as a hobby but she supposed that qualified, particularly if the weather was nice. She wrote all the candidates down in her notebook, determined to get started with at least one when she was back in the city.

That made her think about her job. In theory, she should be in the office tomorrow morning. Which clearly wasn't going to happen since there was no ferry. Even if she was in the office, the small company was privately owned (by Tony since his dad's death). She wasn't sure what would happen to it now. Another question for the morning. She made a list of those too. It was all so exhausting. She eyed the bed. Sadie was stretched out across it diagonally. Was it too early to turn in? She hadn't slept too well the night before despite Sadie's comforting presence. She'd take the dog out and then they'd turn in. Tomorrow was going to be a busy day.

"Sadie?" The dog opened one eye and looked at her without raising her head. "Let's go out and go potty." She tried to sound cheerful, but she wasn't any more enthused about it than the dog was. She held out a small bit of olive, which for some reason Sadie seemed to love. The dog jumped down and followed her out of the room but demanded the treat before going downstairs. In agreement, they went down the steps and Amelia opened the outside door for Sadie, opting to stay in the lobby as it was getting to the gloomy stage of dusk outside. She rubbed her elbows nervously as she waited. The inn staff seemed to be mostly keeping to themselves today, maybe because nobody needed to check in or out, she wasn't sure.

Outside, Ralph came around the corner carrying several black trash bags. He kept going towards where Amelia knew the Dumpsters were located. Then Sadie appeared at the door, her tail wagging. Amelia let her back in and they went back upstairs. She brushed her teeth and repositioned the desk in front of the door. She turned off the lights and went to bed with the smell of slightly damp dog teasing her nostrils.

Chapter 15

☙

Monday morning dawned bright and early. The skies had cleared except for a few inconsequential clouds. Amelia smiled and stretched in her bed. It was going to be a busy day ferreting out answers and finally meeting with the police. Her instinct said she had most of the puzzle pieces, but just hadn't quite fit them all together yet. Of course, one or two things might still be missing. But she was sure with careful attention she could solve this case by the end of the day. Maybe.

She opted not to go into town for breakfast. She wanted to be on the phone with one of those darn lawyers as soon as they started accepting calls. So, she made a pot of coffee in the bathroom and nibbled on the last few cookies. She took Sadie downstairs and found Sara, her face freshly scrubbed, cleaning the lobby. She double-checked the name tag pinned to her chest to make sure it was the same girl. Sara was scowling as she wiped down the windows.

"Excuse us," Amelia said cheerfully as she waited for Sara to stop so she could open the door for Sadie. She did so and then stepped back. "So, Becky said you're saving for college, is that right?"

Sara looked at her with defiant eyes. "So?"

"I'm just interested that's all. It's good to see young women interested in education. What are you thinking about studying?"

"I dunno. Just want off this stupid island," came the sullen reply.

"Oh, I see. So, you don't have a particular college in mind?"

Sara shrugged. "Josh is talking about Washington State, but his grades aren't that good. He'll probably end up at community college."

"Was Josh the boy you were with in town?"

Sara shrugged again. "Probably."

Amelia gave up. "Well, see you later," she said as she let Sadie in and turned to go back to the room. As she did so, she saw Ralph hanging back in the little office behind the reception desk. He had clearly been listening but didn't say anything. He stepped back into the shadows as she passed.

Back in her room, Amelia arranged her temporary computer, notebook, journal and coffee cup on the small table. Her first call was to the office. Jenny, the multi-purpose accountant and office manager, usually got in by 7:30. But Amelia practically had to take a number to reach her. The first five times she called the line was busy. Finally, about an hour later she got through.

"Hey Jenny, it's Amelia."

"What is going on? Tony's fiancée keeps calling me demanding money. Why isn't she on her honeymoon?"

"Didn't she tell you? Tony was murdered on Friday."

"What!! No, she definitely didn't mention that."

"And they aren't allowing anyone on or off the island, by ferry anyway, until the police get here later today."

"So, you're not coming in then."

"Nope. But Jenny, what happens to the business? Did Tony leave a will or something?"

"Noooo. I'm not supposed to tell anyone this but…"

"What?" Dread pooled in Amelia's stomach.

"Heather's daddy bought a controlling interest in the business. It was finalized two weeks ago."

"Good heavens, why? I thought we were making money."

"We are, but Tony was spending more of it. Mr. Hammond paid off his debts but said he wasn't going to keep doing it. And if anything went south in the marriage, Tony would be out of a job."

"Wow. I had no idea. What was he spending it on?"

There was a long pause on the other end of the line. "How much time did you spend in his office?"

"As little as possible."

"So, you didn't see the baggie of cocaine in his top drawer?"

"What! In the office?"

"Just sayin' what I saw. And no, it wasn't sugar for his coffee. One, because we have plenty in the break room, but I also walked in on him doing a line about a month ago."

"Seriously? And you kept this to yourself?"

Jenny sighed. "What good would telling anyone do? They don't arrest people for dealing on the sidewalk in front of the building, what do the police care for one guy consuming it in his office? I updated my resume. I just hadn't decided where to send it yet. Now I don't know. I should probably start sending it out, hunh?"

"Umm, I guess. Crap. What about our retirement?"

"Don't know, hon. Let me know when you're going to be back in. I'll email you if I hear anything from Mr. Hammond, okay?"

"Sure. Hey, can you send it to my personal account? I don't have my regular computer with me."

"Okay. Look the phone's lighting up like crazy. Probably Heather again. I'd better go."

"'K bye."

Amelia pressed off, feeling slightly frozen. Tony had been using. That explained a few things, actually. But not all of them. How had she not seen it? Was it only because she'd made a conscious effort to ignore him as much as possible? Was she ignoring anything important the same way now? And now her dream was in serious jeopardy. She took a few calming gulps of coffee. Maybe the lawyers would have some more cheerful news. She grinned slightly around the mouth of the thick white mug. She was going crazy. Attorneys never had cheerful news to share. She dialed the number anyway.

"Finchley and Patterson." A peppy woman answered the phone.

"Hi. My name is Amelia Feelgood. Someone there transferred a lot of property to my name without my knowledge. I'd like to talk to the person involved."

"Ummm. I see. Ms. Feelgood, do you know the client's name?"

"Try Tony Lyle."

"Oh of course. Mr. Lyle has been working with Mr. Hughes. Let me just see if he's in."

Amelia listened to light jazz for upwards of ten minutes.

"Ms. Feelgood? Dan Hughes. How can I help you?"

"Mr. Hughes, you can explain why the county assessor seems to think I own six pages of real estate without my knowing anything about it."

He hmmed and hawed in her ear for a few minutes. She pictured a portly man who regularly indulged in cigars and referred to his wife as 'the little woman'.

"Tony said he explained everything."

"Well, he lied. He never said a word."

"Perhaps you should talk with him first."

"That's going to be a little difficult, Mr. Hughes, without a seance. He's dead."

The genial condescension dropped from his voice. "What?" his voice cracked. "What happened?"

"He was murdered sometime on Friday. Now, why am I listed as the owner on this property?"

"Are you sure about that?"

"Quite. I saw the body. It's still in the same place it was on Friday. Not even Tony could fake it for that long."

"Um sure. I'll need to confirm this with the police first. Do you have a case number?"

Amelia sighed. "The police are coming later today. It's a long story. You can call the sheriff." She rattled off his number, not caring if the sheriff didn't want to be contacted by lawyers. He must be used to it by now and it was his own fault for not getting someone out here all weekend. "You can at least explain to me how this is even possible without my consent."

"Totally legal. Doesn't happen too often, you understand, but giving someone something doesn't require their signature. You could refuse to pay the taxes and then it would revert to the county, but transferring it doesn't require permission."

"Great. And now that he's dead?"

"I really can't divulge client information, but if he is dead and you didn't transfer the property back to him or anyone else, then you own it free and clear."

Amelia caught her own gaze in the mirror opposite the table. Her eyes were wide with shock. She owned over half the island. Whether she wanted to or not.

℗

When she had partially recovered from the shock, Amelia paced the room a bit, checked her phone for messages and generally dithered for a few hours. She wasn't particularly surprised that Mr. Hughes never called her back. There was more than one way to get information. She called Sheriff Harrison. She was a little surprised when he picked up.

"Harrison."

"Sheriff. I'm assuming an annoying lawyer has called you this morning."

"Which one? My days are full of annoying lawyers."

"Mr. Hughes. Tony Lyle's attorney."

"Oh him. Yeah, what about it?"

"He wouldn't tell me why I suddenly own all this property even though it was done without my consent. He hasn't called me back now that he's confirmed Tony is dead, so I'm hoping you'll tell me what he told you."

"Uh, that's confidential..."

"It's my business, Sheriff. Do you want me to file a freedom of information request and go to the local news? Because I'll do it. Something is fishy and I have a right to know how I'm involved."

He sighed heavily. "Why did I even get up this morning? All right, but off the record. I haven't confirmed any of this."

Amelia smiled with satisfaction and sat down with her notebook and pen at the ready.

"Apparently Tony was concerned about his divorce not having been completely legal."

"Okay. What does that have to do with me?"

"You're just a bystander. One he thought he could manipulate."

"Great," she mumbled under her breath.

"He wanted the property out of his legal possession but close by until he was sure his ex couldn't claim it. Then he was going to have you sign off to transfer it back to him."

"How… cozy."

"Makes you a wealthy woman."

"I didn't kill him, Sheriff."

"Didn't say you did. For what it's worth, Gus doesn't think you did either."

"Hunh. Nice to know."

"We'll have a team out there this afternoon."

"Goody. All right. Thanks for your time, Sheriff."

Amelia doodled in her notebook. Maybe the property was completely separate from Tony's murder. Or maybe it wasn't. The only person with a motive there would be her, and she knew she hadn't done it. Unless someone still thought Tony owned it all? Then who would benefit from his death? His ex-wife who might not be fully an ex? Maybe. And she was secretly on the island and in the inn. And why had he kept one falling-down property back, still under his name? Did he think it was so run down that his ex wouldn't want it? Ugh, she couldn't process all the possibilities. Maybe she and Sadie should go into the village for lunch so they'd be well fortified for the police when they finally got here.

Sadie approved of the idea, so Amelia grabbed her jacket and they headed out. The golf cart she had been using was gone, so she had to use the next one in the little corral. Everyone must have decided to go out this morning because it was the next to the last one available. She backed it out of the awkward angle it had been left in but before she could pull out of the drive, Sadie was scratching at the vinyl seat. "Sadie! Stop that. I think we actually own this." Sadie just barked and kept digging at the seam between the seat and the back, absently like something was interesting but not exciting. She stopped as soon as Amelia inserted her fingers in the gap, delighted that a human was finally noticing. Amelia slid her fingers through, not sure what had Sadie so interested. Her fingers finally hit something hard, like a book. She levered it out of the seam. It was one of those thin high-school romance paperbacks. It looked in poor reading taste but innocuous enough. She showed it to Sadie, who just settled down and smiled. Amelia plopped it down on the passenger side footwell, but as she did so the pages opened and she saw a note folded inside. Reaching over to grab it, her foot slipped off the break and they did a slow roll towards the Dumpster.

"Crap!" She hurriedly turned the steering wheel and then brought the cart to a halt. Maybe she'd better just turn it off while she checked this out.

She unfolded the small rectangle of white paper. "Sara, Come see me in room 236 this evening to discuss. I'm sure you now see why you'll want to be my special friend. TL." There was a small photo that had been printed out on plain paper cut and taped to the note. It showed Sara taking a small duffel bag into the old mansion in the woods where Amelia had just been yesterday.

Chapter 16

❦

Amelia pondered that note deeply as she and Sadie headed into town for lunch. The sullen teenager was clearly hiding something, more than what the nasty attitude was meant to cover. And Tony was utter slime. But that part wasn't exactly news. Each day he seemed to have sunk to a new low, which was kind of amazing considering how dead he was. There was one person that might be able to shed some light on it. Her spine tingled a little, with excitement or fear she wasn't too sure.

She kept driving through the village. She drove through the workers' village of Shin's Landing. She pondered the amazing greenness of moss as she continued on to the narrow rural road. At the big carved sign surrounded by no trespassing signs, she turned. When the driveway climbed over a small hill, she stopped the golf cart and gasped. It was a perfect little fairy tale cottage with slumping thatched roof and higgledy-piggledy windows. It was adorable and she half turned her head to look for Snow White. What she got was a solid menacing man standing completely still in the clearing to the left with his unblinking gaze on her.

"Oh, there you are, Gus. Good. I have a question."

"Do those signs mean nothing?" he inquired calmly.

"What signs? Oh those. Well, no. I'm not trespassing. I'm here to find you. Why were you just standing there?"

"Because I knew you were coming. You're lucky I could see who it was."

He was teasing, surely. But there were no laugh lines present. "Are you psychic?" she asked, genuinely curious.

Clearly, he hadn't expected that. His shoulders relaxed with his sigh. "Cameras, Ms. Feelgood."

"Oh! Then maybe you really can help."

"With what, precisely?"

She got out of the cart, feeling in her bag for the note. She had to stop and pull it open before fishing the paper out of the bottom of the bag. "I found this in the golf cart. I thought maybe you'd know what she's carrying and why it's a big deal." Reluctantly, she handed it to Gus. He scanned it.

"Is the girl Sara?"

"Yeah, do you know her?"

"No, just going by the name in the note. It's drugs, probably cocaine."

"How on earth can you tell that? I thought you might have seen some of this activity."

He didn't answer her question. "You and Sadie might as well come in." He led the way into the most charming house Amelia had ever seen. Inside was a different story. The charm was still there in terms of the architecture, but it was clear Gus wasn't exactly nesting. Plain, sturdy furniture dotted the downstairs open plan. Not a pillow, plant or piece of art in sight.

"I was in the middle of lunch, want something?" His offer wasn't ungracious exactly, more rusty from disuse.

Amelia pondered. "What are you having?"

"Mushroom ravioli with garlic bread."

"And you have extra?"

"Yeah, I was going to save it for tomorrow, but you can have it if you want."

"That sounds good, thanks."

He looked surprised that she accepted, but she brazened him out. He turned and led the way into the kitchen which was just darn cute.

"If you don't mind me saying, this house doesn't really seem to be what you'd go for."

"What do you think I go for?" He sounded genuinely curious.

"Practical. Maybe an apartment over a giant workshop. Or a log cabin in the woods."

"Well, I'd have taken the latter, yeah. I wanted privacy - this was the only place available."

He put a plate of pasta down in front of her and handed her some silverware. She took a quick nibble. "Ohh, this is really good. Where'd you get it."

"Made it."

"Seriously?"

"Seriously. I'm trying to slow down and take up a hobby."

"Hey, me too!"

"So back to your drug mule…"

"My what?"

"Mule - someone who moves the merchandise from point A to point B."

"Oh. Yes?"

He held up his large square hands as those holding a small package.

"That's what packages typically look like when they're not concealed. It's almost exactly a kilo, relatively easy to be discreet as long as nobody is looking too closely."

"And they're using the old house as a transfer point."

"That's what the photo seems to be saying."

"So that white powder I saw in there was..?"

"What white powder? You didn't mention it yesterday."

"No, well it didn't seem important then. There was some whitish stuff inside the oven box of the old wood stove in the kitchen. I kinda thought it was ash of some kind, but it was a little too white. Plus, I don't think anyone's had a fire in there in fifty years, but I wasn't thinking about drugs."

Gus shrugged. "I'll take a look. If it is the police can swing by while they're here. I take it TL is Tony?"

"I'm assuming so. That's his room number."

"Putz."

"No argument here."

"Are they here yet?"

"Who?" She swiveled her head around looking for what she wasn't sure.

Gus started laughing. "The police. On the island. Not the aliens."

"Oh. I don't know. I talked to the sheriff this morning. He said after lunch."

"Hmmm. Well, it's just about that now. When you're done there, I'll follow you back and have a chat about this." He put the note in his pocket before Amelia could ask for it back.

"So, what were you talking to Harrison about, anyway?"

"The whole property thing. Stupid lawyer wouldn't tell me, client privacy and all that, but he was perfectly willing to blab to the sheriff. So, I called him and convinced him to tell me."

"You did?"

"Yes. I did threaten him with media coverage, but all in all, he caved pretty easy."

"What did you learn?"

"Tony was trying to get away with something and transferred all the land to me, thinking he could get it back without me knowing when he was ready. Get me to sign something thinking it was a different document or something. In any event, since he's quite dead and can't do that now, it seems it's mine. Unless some new complication crops up, which I'm fully expecting."

"Nice windfall."

"Not really. I was just waiting to vest in my retirement and then I was moving to France. Now I don't know what I'm doing."

"Why France?"

She ate her last bite of pasta. "Because it's where I'm meant to be. I've always known that. The French have flair."

"Can't argue there. You ever been?"

"No."

"You were planning to move to a foreign country that you've never visited."

"Still planning. I haven't given up hope."

He rose from his chair shaking his head slowly. "Ms. Feelgood, I'm not sure France is ready for you."

Well, what the heck did that mean?

He waved her through to the front door. "I'll catch up to you on the road."

"Um okay. I can wait."

"Please don't. That golf cart can't go above a crawl. I'll have to practically walk behind you."

Amelia shrugged and got back in the maligned golf cart with Sadie and headed back up the road. A few minutes later, the throaty growl of an engine was behind her. She slowed and turned her head. Gus was on a sleek black motorcycle, perfectly tended and without an ounce of chrome anywhere to be seen. His bald head was bare to the sky. She stopped the golf cart and got out.

Walking back to him, she pointed at his head. "You need to wear a helmet!"

He rolled his eyes. "Not for walking behind that grocery cart, I don't."

"That grocery cart isn't moving until it's on."

"You're kidding right?"

She put her hands on her hips and stared him down. Sadie woofed from her seat enthusiastically.

"Oh, good god. All right." He unstrapped a black helmet with a darkened visor from the side and put it on, adjusting the chin strap. "Happy now?"

"Yes. Thank you." She knew better than to gloat in her victory but there was a certain satisfied swing to her hips as she went back to the golf cart and climbed in. She periodically checked her rear-view mirror to see if he still had it on and if he was actually walking the powerful machine.

When they arrived at the inn it was clear that the police had finally made it. A covered gurney was waiting in the drive watched over by a young technician. That must be Tony, she thought, finally on his way to the morgue. Amelia had to just park the golf cart wherever she could because the access to the corral was blocked by various vehicles. None of them were police cars, but she supposed if they'd arrived by boat, then they would have had to borrow something locally. Was there an island rental she was unaware of? The golf cart had been fun at first, but it was getting old. She wouldn't mind a better set of wheels.

Gus followed her inside, still glowering at her slightly.

"What are you upset about? It's not like you need to worry about your hair."

He glowered harder.

Inside the cops had requisitioned the little library as an interview room while various people came and went from the upstairs. Several guests were clustered around partly for the entertainment factor and also to pester anyone in uniform about when they could go home.

"I'll catch up with you later," Gus murmured close to her ear before going to the library door and knocking as he opened it. He closed the door behind him.

"Ma'am? Are you a guest here?" a young officer asked her.

"Yes."

"We're asking everyone to please stay in their rooms so we can do this as fast as possible. We have a guest list, so we'll call your room if we have questions."

"Oh, okay. Well, how do I get upstairs then? There seems to be a lot of activity."

"I'll take you through, ma'am. Is that your dog?"

"Sort of."

"And you don't have a leash?" he sounded disapproving.

"No, she's not completely my dog. That's the part that isn't."

He looked confused but didn't argue. He led the way through the equipment lined up in the hall. Upstairs was fairly clear.

"Thanks." She waved him back downstairs while she and Sadie went into the room. She immediately went to the window and peered down to see what she could see. It looked like they'd already combed through the area pretty thoroughly.

Chapter 17

ℰℑ

"Sadie, we forgot to get more food," Amelia announced with
dismay when she turned away from the window. Sadie seemed
unconcerned, stationing herself in front of the bureau drawer where
the last can of dog food was stored. She'd been so distracted by Gus
on his motorcycle, she'd forgotten to stop in town and restock. But
maybe it didn't matter. Maybe they could get out of here tomorrow.
She looked over at Sadie. No, not 'we'. Sadie belonged on the island.
If Amelia left, it would just be her. Panic rose in the back of her
throat when she realized she'd unconsciously used the word 'if'.

"Not if, when," she said firmly.

To renew her resolve, she got out her phone and forced herself to
do fifteen minutes of French lessons. It was torture. She didn't give
a damn if Paul had a big kitchen (Paul a une cuisine grande) or that
Marie and Isabel often traveled together (Marie et Isabel voyagent
ensemble souvent). That really seemed like Marie and Isabel's personal
business. What Amelia was preoccupied with was who the heck had
killed Tony. She almost had it. There were just a couple of things that
didn't quite add up. And now there were police everywhere, which
was going to make it harder to tie up those last little details.

As if she'd conjured them up, her room phone rang. The nice
officer requested her presence in the library downstairs. Amelia's
hands started sweating. Why she wasn't sure. She knew she hadn't
killed Tony, but Heather had done a lot of rumor spreading in the
last few days. She looked around the room to make sure it was dog-

proofed for an hour or two. She slid some of the papers into a drawer and put the books up on top of the TV, then grabbed her cell phone. Sadie seemed unconcerned and uninterested in following her. She was spread out on the floor, looking dead. Amelia stepped over her and left the room.

It took her a few minutes to navigate the police techs that had moved upstairs. She had to place one hand on the rose-color wallpaper to sort of jump over one or two of the techs but eventually, she made it to the stairwell. Then she was standing in the open door to the library facing a stern-faced uniformed officer. "Ms. Feelgood?"

"Yes, that's me."

"Come in, have a seat. I understand you worked for Mr. Lyle."

"I did, yes."

"And you own the inn?"

"Apparently."

"Doesn't it make any money?"

She huffed. "If you've done your research then you know that I didn't know anything about it until this weekend. Clearly Tony was up to something nefarious, but he didn't tell me about it."

"So, you were angry?"

"I am now, but I didn't know any of this until after he was dead."

"Why would owning a significant property portfolio make you angry?"

"I don't need the headache. I'm planning to move to France within the year."

"Why would you feel the need to flee the country?"

"I'm not fleeing! I haven't done anything wrong!"

"Hmmm."

Amelia had had enough. "Have you watched all of the security footage?"

The officer sat up abruptly. "What footage?"

"From the security cameras - it's all on that machine there." She pointed through the closed library door towards the reception lobby.

"Bateman!" the officer called sharply. Another officer opened the door and stepped in. "We'll continue this later, Ms. Feelgood."

Amelia smirked ever so slightly to herself. She'd thought that would work and now she had an opening to answer one of her dangling questions. She led Officer Bateman out to the reception computer and then stood back where she could still see the screen. It came up on the password lock screen but not before it showed the date and time. Amelia discreetly glanced down at her phone screen. The computer was a full hour ahead.

Officer Bateman turned to her, "Unlock it, please."

"Oh, I don't have the password. You'll need one of the hotel staff for that. I'll just go see, shall I?"

She stepped away and into the little back room that seemed to hide all the staff activity. Sara was huddled in the office chair clasping her elbows and scowling. "Oh Sara, hi. Do you know the password for the lobby computer? The police need it."

If anything, she scowled harder. "No, I just clean. You'll need Uncle Ralph or Becky for that."

"Are they around?"

She shrugged "Dunno."

Amelia rolled her eyes. "Why are you hanging out back here?"

"Can't exactly clean anything, can I? Why aren't they just thanking whoever whacked that slimeball and leaving us to get on with things? What do they care?"

"Was Tony blackmailing you, Sara?"

"No. I don't have any money."

Amelia thought back to the note she'd found. 'Special friend' didn't exactly imply a financial payout. She opened her mouth to ask about that, but Sara jumped up when an officer appeared in the doorway. "I have to go." And the girl ran out.

The officer looked at Amelia. "The password," he said sternly.

"I'm told either Ralph or Becky have it. Maybe you know where one of them is?"

As if on cue, Ralph came into the reception from outside. The office pounced. "Sir, can you unlock this work station?" Amelia watched from the side. Ralph hadn't even noticed her, yet but he was nervous. He ran his tongue over his lips and didn't make eye contact with the officer. "Uh, sure. Is there something you're looking for?"

"We were told there's security camera footage on this machine."

Ralph looked shocked and then his whole body slumped slightly. He went over to the machine and typed something in and then stepped back. Leaning against the wall, he closed his eyes.

The officer clicked around and took a thumb drive from his chest pocket. Amelia was impressed, considering how long it had taken her to remember she had one. She decided to throw one more cat in with the pigeons. "Ralph?"

He opened his eyes, seeming to notice her for the first time.

"I noticed the computer time clock is off by an hour. Do you know why that is?" The officer's eyes widened and he looked down at the screen. Then he pulled out his notebook and wrote something down. Ralph looked blank for a minute, then he said, "Daylight savings or is it standard? Either way, it's too old to change automatically, so we just let it be."

"So for six months, the clock is wrong?"

Ralph just shrugged.

Amelia looked over at the policeman. "Are you guys staying over? Do you need rooms?"

He looked at her like he knew she was trying to change the subject. "No. We're taking the body back tonight. If we need more, we'll come back tomorrow."

"Oh! Does that mean the ferry can run again?"

He shrugged "Not my call."

He pulled out the thumb drive and put it back in his pocket, then made some more notes in his little notebook. Amelia wondered if he watched a lot of cop shows on TV. He looked young enough that he should be typing most of his notes into his phone, surely?

It was getting on towards dinner time and since she hadn't stopped for food, she was going to have to head into town, or at least as far as lentils. She thought about that for a minute. No, she wasn't desperate enough to save the ten minutes into the village proper. She went back to the library door where the officers were starting to pack up. "Gentlemen, if it's all right with you, I'm going to head into the village for dinner. We're done here, right?"

"For now. Have a nice night."

"Thanks," she answered dryly. "Do either of you know anything about the ferry resuming service? I have guests who want to leave."

Both of them shrugged. "Pretty much up to the sheriff on that one."

Amelia sighed. In a day or two, she'd know Sheriff Harrison better than her next-door neighbor. "Fine. I'll call him in the morning."

As if a school bell had rung, all of the officers and techs were assembling their gear and notes and congregating in the front drive. Amelia watched, bemused, as someone starting rolling the gurney down the drive towards the ferry dock. Out of nowhere, Gus appeared at her side, making her jump.

She squeaked. "What are you, a vampire?"

He didn't bother to answer, so she continued with her real question. "Where are they going with him?"

"Down to the dock. They parked the boat over at Shin's Landing. Someone is bringing it around."

"Do you know when the ferry can start running again?"

He looked down at her sardonically. "Eager to leave us?"

"I do have a job to get back to you know."

"Hmmm." He paused for several seconds. "Probably Wednesday."

She stood there silently, looking at the men and women chatting in the drive while they waited for some signal to move out.

"I know who did it."

She saw him whip his head around, scanning the room, then he grabbed her upper arm in a tight grip. "Do you actually have a death wish? Not here!"

It was precisely because she didn't have a death wish that she'd said something. It felt safer somehow for someone else to know, preferably the police, but they didn't seem quite ready to listen. It was hard to tell if Gus was taking her seriously either. His cell phone rang and he answered it without saying a word. Amelia felt that spooky shiver tickle her spine. He stepped away from her, turning his back, said a single "yes" into the phone and hung up.

"I have to go," he said to her. "Stay out of trouble. In fact, stay in your room, and put something heavy in front of the door."

"I need food."

He sighed. "Get takeout from the pub. Don't be alone with anyone right now got it?"

She didn't. This seemed bigger than Tony. Obviously, his murderer had been on the loose for days now and nobody had told her to barricade herself in her room. She narrowed her eyes at him and flipped the sharp edge of her haircut. "Why?"

"I don't have time or clearance to discuss that with you right now."

Strangely that shut up all the arguments she'd had stockpiled for just such an occasion. "Fine. I'm taking Sadie with me to the pub." She turned and left, heading upstairs to do exactly that.

Chapter 18

❧

Amelia decided that if she and Sadie were going to risk death by not immediately barricading themselves in the room, then she was going to go all out. They cruised into town in the golf cart. She'd intended to stop at the wine shop by the Vegi Heaven first but there was some kind of party going on in the cafe and all the available parking spots were taken. Fine, she'd stop at the snobby wine shop in the village and see if she could piss off that guy even more. Maybe she'd ask for a discount blend. She grinned evilly to herself only just catching sight of a group of tourists stepping back on the sidewalk and whispering to themselves when they saw her. She resumed her normal expression.

She stopped first at the grocery store and stocked up on the staples, including dog food and treats. Sadie panted happily when Amelia put the bags into the footwell of the golf cart. "You know, Sadie, I'm going to have to go back to the city soon. You might want to figure out your next home." Sadie lay down on the seat and closed her eyes. Familiar with avoiding things you didn't quite want to hear, Amelia just smiled and drove them to the snooty wine shop. She was almost done with the first wine box, not that she felt a need to admit that to anyone. Her plans to put the proprietor in his place were foiled though when the only staff were two nice young women who didn't mind pointing her to the boxed wine section in the slightest. Heather came in just as Amelia was reaching for her wallet at the checkout. She gripped her brother's arm as though trying to pull him in front of her. "What are you doing here? Didn't the police arrest you?"

The young woman ringing Amelia up paused for a second, then shrugged and continued with the transaction.

"No Heather, they didn't." She smiled benignly and went back to her golf cart. It hadn't occurred to her until Gus mentioned it that the pub would do takeout, but she'd been anticipating it ever since. She would load up with a hearty dinner and something for Sadie and then they would indeed shut themselves in come hell or high water, possibly both.

The pub was doing a brisk business, so Amelia left Sadie in charge of the golf cart and went in, bypassing the cluster of people waiting for a table. "I heard I can order takeout, is that okay?" she asked the woman at the till. "Sure, here's a menu. Just let me know when you're ready."

Feeling like it just might be her last hot meal for a while, she studied carefully. There was a tingle at the base of her spine like she was being watched. When she peeked over her shoulder, she saw Ralph, Sara and Sara's dad sitting at a table by the wall. Sara's back was to her, but she could see the girl was picking at her nails. Ralph quickly looked down at his menu.

"I'll have the extra-large burger with fries, please. Oh, and can you do a patty or something for Sadie?" she asked the hostess.

"Hey, no problem." She rang it up and Amelia handed her a credit card. "Ten minutes, okay?"

"That's fine. I'll just wait outside." She escaped to the golf cart, leaning a hip on the seat and looking around the square. It was a lot quieter midweek, even though all the same tourists were still confined to the island. The excitement had definitely worn off. A young waiter brought her food out to her in a large paper sack. Amelia rolled it up tight to protect it from Sadie's inquiring nose and stowed it in the footwell.

"Ready? Let's get out of here."

They hurried back, Amelia pushing the golf cart to its maximum speed, which wasn't particularly fast. In part, she didn't want her

French fries getting cold and part was instinct and that spot between her shoulder blades that was not at all happy.

That feeling only increased when they got to the inn. There was nobody about. The lobby was empty as was the stairwell. Sadie rushed into the room and declared it all clear with a happy bark as Amelia followed behind with the bags. She dumped everything on the bed but then moved the pub sack to the table when Sadie starting pushing her snout enthusiastically under the edges. First things first, though. She moved the desk in front of the door. Then she found something to watch on TV, as luck would have it a home renovation show set in France. Thankfully it was all in English and Amelia stood there transfixed at the blue-tiled turret that looked like it belonged in Disneyland. Only this one was real.

Sadie brought her back to the present with an insistent paw on her hip administered from the edge of the bed. Amelia dished up dinner, delighted to find that the fries were still warm. Sadie gulped down her burger patty before Amelia had even sat down, but wasn't pushy about having more. She curled up on the bed with her head between her paws and sighed like the world was going to end at any minute.

When a knock came at the door Amelia wondered if it wasn't.

"Ms. Feelgood? There's a phone call for you in the office," Sara called out. Amelia got up out of habit and then paused. She looked over at the beige phone by the bed. No light was blinking. "I'm not dressed. Can you transfer it to the room?"

"Oh! Um, yeah I guess so." Footsteps receded. Amelia looked over at the phone, somehow knowing it wasn't going to ring. She put two fries in her mouth and bit down viciously. She turned her attention back to the TV show. It was only as the credits were rolling that she was reminded that the phone, in fact, had not rung, despite Sara's acknowledgment. She almost felt insulted at the weak lure. Surely they could do better?

Of course, as soon as she realized she really couldn't leave her room safely until morning, a million and one things occurred to her that she really needed to do outside of it. She distracted herself by turning the lights out and then going to the window to see if she could see the stars. It was cloudy so she couldn't, but she did see the flash of a cell phone as someone outside moved it away from their face. A few minutes, later she heard the unmistakable click of a key card being inserted in her door lock. Sadie sat up and started growling low and deep in her throat. The desk held. Whoever it was retreated, leaving the door open about half an inch. Amelia crawled up on the desk to shut it again and then added some of the bureau drawers on top for extra weight. She got into bed, the lights still out and her body on high alert until she fell into a fitful sleep.

ↄ⁀ↄ

Amelia woke exhausted from tensing at every little sound during the night. But everything looked safer in the daylight and she was pleased to see that the clouds had cleared. It took a few minutes to undo all her safety precautions, but then she headed downstairs with Sadie to let the dog out. The lobby was once again empty, but there was an expectant hush. Even the birds outside were being quieter than normal. Sadie rushed after one of the wild rabbits and Amelia stepped into a patch of sunshine to wait for her return. She needed coffee.

Her reverie was disturbed by the unexpected, naturally. A group of about ten men in white uniforms with some bits of gold braid here and there were walking down the road two by two. They were coming from the village or at least that direction and headed to either the inn or the ferry dock. Wherever they were going they kept their focus there, looking neither to the right or the left. Amelia watched them walk by, curiosity getting the better of her as she checked out their rear ends to see if they had visible panty lines on the white pants. They didn't. She wondered what the secret was and if it was something she could find online. She was not prepared to jog after them to ask. Sadie came bouncing up, so Amelia turned to go back inside. It was time to call the sheriff since there didn't seem to be any police about. She didn't think she was up to making a citizen's arrest without someone to turn the criminal over to.

She made a pot of coffee despite being sick of the hotel version—it just never tasted quite right—and sat down with her cell phone. It didn't have a great signal, but she couldn't risk using the room phone. She found the slip of paper with the sheriff's number and considered whether she should save it to her address book on her phone. Having the police on speed dial did not seem like the direction she wanted for her life. If she had reason to call him after today then she would. That decided she punched in the number and waited.

"Harrison." He sounded tired like he hadn't slept at all.

"Sheriff? It's Amelia Feelgood."

There was a long pause and then a sigh that lasted almost as long.

"Ms. Feelgood, yes, you can have your ferry back today. Yes, you can leave. We'll be out later today to make an arrest."

"Oh, that is good news! What time do you think someone will be here to arrest him?"

"Him? Who do you think did it?"

"Why Ralph, of course. Who were you thinking it was?"

"I can't tell you that. That's why we're the cops. Now tell me why you think it's Ralph." He sounded tired but intrigued, so she laid it out for him.

"His niece, Sara, is a drug mule." Another long pause. Amelia was expecting him to be shocked and ask questions but he didn't. She assumed that's because he already knew that part.

"Tony was using cocaine."

"What about Ralph, Ms. Feelgood?"

"I'm getting to that. Tony was using and caught Sara dropping a shipment at the big house in the woods. Which he owned, by the way."

"Go on. But if you could get to the point before noon, I'd appreciate it."

"Is that when? Oh, never mind. Anyway, Tony then blackmailed Sara or tried to for sex and drugs in exchange for not saying anything. The drug people were already sending prostitutes his way in order to keep him out of the way while they moved the drugs. Apparently, if a woman showed up at his door offering sex, Tony didn't bother asking questions. Sara is young and stupid, so she was going to go along with it. Probably too scared to think of any other options."

Another long pause from the sheriff. "Keep going."

"Ralph walked in on them in Tony's room before too much happened."

"And then he killed him?"

"No of course not, that would have been too obvious. No, he got Sara out of there and then he went back when she cleaned the room and unlocked the French doors. Then he came around from the service door to the patio when he knew Tony was there, made sure the camera was out of range, and went in through that side."

"Do you have any proof of this?"

"Yes. It's all in the video footage if you remember to take off the hour for daylight savings that they never bother to adjust. Oh, and the blackmail note that I gave to Gus, which presumably you have, right?"

"I'm aware of the note."

"You don't sound happy, sheriff."

"I've never seen an island go from zero to sixty in crime so fast. I'll make a few calls, that's all I can say, Ms. Feelgood. But if I were you, I'd stay in my room."

"Until when, sheriff? I do have to eat, you know."

"We'll have someone out there this afternoon."

And he hung up. Well crap, Amelia thought to herself. She couldn't tell if he'd believed her or not, but she was worried that her theory was news. She knew she was right. But who had they planned to arrest instead of Ralph?

Chapter 19

❧

It was anybody's guess really as to who the police had initially suspected of Tony's murder. Ten hours after her phone call with Sheriff Harrison, Amelia was seated cross-legged on her bed with a glass of wine and a bowl of popcorn. She was watching the evening news out of Seattle as they talked about the big drug bust on Findlater Island. More than twenty people were arrested by a joint task force of the sheriff's department, the Coast Guard (that's who they were!), and the FBI. They'd been under observation for months, but the murder of a respected businessman (Amelia snorted) had kicked off the takedown. Amelia finally got to see Sheriff Harrison as he took the podium at the press conference. He was good looking in a rough and tumble sort of way, but the brown uniform wasn't as snappy as the Coast Guard's. She wondered if he was open to a little fashion advice? He was rubbing his hand over his face like he was trying to stay awake as reporters started asking questions. Maybe she should wait a week or two before discussing flair with the sheriff.

She still didn't know if Ralph had been arrested, but then finally the FBI guy took the microphone and a picture of Ralph flashed up on the screen. But his name wasn't really Ralph. It was Emilio Cortez and he'd been hiding out from a drug cartel for the last twenty years. Sara was only his niece by marriage and Ralph had been far more motivated about making sure the cartel didn't find him through Tony's loose lips than anything else. "Well, I'll be," Amelia said to Sadie, who thumped her tail lightly.

"Did you know any of this, Sadie?" Sadie rolled over and showed her tummy. Amelia reached out and gave it a thorough rub.

Amelia got off the bed and took her dishes into the bathroom. She wasn't willing to take any chances until she could get on the ferry tomorrow, so she pushed the desk in front of the door again. For old time's sake, if nothing else. Her bags were packed. "Who's going to take them down to the ferry for me, Sadie? Heck, who's working at the hotel besides Becky? She can't do it all." Crap. And since it was her hotel, it was also her problem. Not that she needed a drug cartel murderer on staff, but still.

"I need a vacation," she announced to the room.

In the morning she took her bags and Sadie down to the lobby. Everyone in the hotel was there trying to check out. Becky was running back and forth to the back room where the printer was and trying to tell people they would have to wheel their own luggage down to the ferry. Her eyes were red-rimmed from crying.

When it was Amelia's turn, Becky's eyes widened. "you're leaving?"

"I've got a real job, Becky. I need to get back to it. Is there something wrong? Besides the lack of staff?"

"My boyfriend, Jack. They arrested him," she said quietly.

"Maybe they made a mistake? Bound to be one or two in something that big…"

"No. Deep down, I knew. I just didn't want to see it."

"I'm sorry."

"Yeah, well. Me too."

"So, I'll get the property thing sorted, okay? I still don't think I really own it for real, but while I do, if Mr. Jain shows up, feel free to offer him his job back. Okay?"

"Okay. That'll help." She smiled slightly.

"I'll call you in a day or so, let you know where things stand."

"Okay." Becky was still hustling as more people had gathered behind Amelia. She got out of the way and took Sadie out to the drive for their goodbyes. "Sadie, thanks for being my sidekick. Take care of yourself, okay?" Sadie just stood there and whined in that eerie high-pitched way that dogs know is annoying but can be heard for half a mile. Amelia's eyes were feeling a little stingy as she put her tote bag on her shoulder and then grabbed the grocery sacks she'd stuffed all her additional purchases into. She walked slowly down the hill towards the ferry, part of a crowd of people ready to say goodbye to the island. In the waiting area, she kept to herself after buying her ticket. It was hard to believe she was leaving now, as though she had no real connection with the island anymore.

It was time to get back to her condo, her job, and her plans for France. If she stayed on track and Findlater Island didn't become the anchor that dragged her down, in a year she should be sipping rosé in the Dordogne admiring little stone cottages with window boxes full of red geraniums.

❧

With the exception of the excited tourist chatter from those that had been trapped on the island, the ferry ride home was uneventful. Amelia sat on the worn vinyl bench seat and watched the evergreen-covered islands pass as they headed towards the city. The boat still had two stops to make so eventually she took out her phone and did a few French lessons, but her heart wasn't really in it. She kept thinking about Sadie out in the rain. Would the next person feed her properly? Would they talk to her like she was a person? She knew they probably would. That was the magic Sadie brought to Findlater but already she was missing the dog at her side.

When they finally docked in Seattle, Amelia joined the throngs walking the covered passage to the terminal and then headed out into a light rain. She ducked her head to keep it off her face as she headed up the hill to her small condominium, pulling her roller case behind her. The entire world was gray, from the sky to the pavement. Amelia unlocked her front door and was surprised to see it looked just like it had when she'd left it. Somehow so much had happened that she'd half expected to find it ransacked or otherwise looking as disturbed and as out of sorts as she felt.

Somewhere high in the heavens was a shoe that hadn't yet dropped. A sense of fate and foreboding had her curled up on her small love seat with the last of the chocolate ice cream from her freezer. It was over. Tony was dead, his murderer caught, and now life could get back to normal. Maybe.

She found the falling shoe the next morning. She went into work a little early, knowing there would be a raft of emails to sort through and plenty of people desperate to gossip about what had happened to Tony. She was surprised therefore when she swiped her key card to open the office suite door to find Jenny at the front desk making horrified motions at her. Then Heather waltzed through in a bright pink suit. The jacket came nowhere near covering her ample bust but instead drew attention to that fact with bold rhinestone buttons. She smirked when she saw Amelia. "Thought you could get away with it, didn't you?"

Amelia still had no idea what she was talking about, so she just shrugged and made her way to her office, which was really just a glass cubicle since it didn't have a window to the outside. Before she could even put down her tote bag, an efficient looking woman was in the doorway. "Ms. Feelgood, can you come with me please?"

"Who are you?"

"I'm Emily. Mr. Hammond's personal assistant."

Ah, Amelia thought to herself. The man with the controlling interest. And... Heather's daddy. Emily left her at the door to the big corner office, the one that had been Tony's just last week. A large man with just a fringe of brown hair at the tops of his ears was seated uncomfortably in the massage chair Tony had used at his desk. Sweat stains were already decorating the underarms of his white dress shirt. "Ah, Ms. Feelgood, I presume?" he said as he looked up.

"Yes?" she answered. He waved at someone else in the office who stood up and came towards her holding out a manila envelope.

"Ms. Amelia Feelgood?" the second man asked.

"Yes," she said more firmly this time.

"You've been served." He handed her the envelope and walked out of the office and down the hall towards the lobby and the exit.

Amelia studied the brown envelope. "What's this about??" she asked the man at the desk.

"Oh, well, now. We've got to get a few things sorted now, don't we? I think we both know you're not entitled to all that island property. Don't know what game you cooked up with Tony, but he was easily led."

"I knew nothing about the property until after his death."

"So you say, so you say," he responded jovially. "I'm sure you understand that with the firm's reputation at stake, you can't continue to work here."

"Wait, you're firing me? Because you're suing me?"

"Well um, not sure I'd put it like that exactly but close enough. Emily here will help you pack up your desk. Be sure you don't try to take any company property. Wouldn't want to have that on your record." He smiled like he was being cute. Amelia thought back to what she'd left on her desk. A sickly plant she didn't particularly like, a coffee mug from last year's white elephant gift exchange and that was about it. When Tony had started snooping through files, she'd taken her personal things home.

"Oh, no need. You can have it all." She smiled sweetly.

"But, but..." he blustered. Had he been planning some sort of gotcha moment?

"And I'll be discussing a counter-suit for wrongful dismissal with my attorney, so is this the address you'd like him to use?"

Mr. Hammond's jaw raised and lowered like the ferry dock trying to align with the boat, but never quite connected.

Inside her own head, Amelia was saying all the bad words she knew in French over and over (because she really didn't know very many). This was not good. It wasn't hard to visualize her savings going towards a high-priced lawyer defending her on these trumped-up charges. She looked down at the manila envelope in her hands. Maybe it would make for amusing reading since she now had the day off. And tomorrow and... She refocused on Mr. Hammond's bald head. "I'm serious, Mr. Hammond, I'm going to head downstairs now to my lawyer so is this where I should tell him he can find you?"

"You can't do that!"

"Why not? He's not the firm's lawyer. He just rents space in the same building. Perfectly legal and ethical."

"Because, because..."

Amelia could now see where Heather got it from. "Because you thought I'd be so scared I'd just sign some papers?"

His flush gave away the answer

"Not going to happen."

She turned and walked towards the entrance, giving Jenny a hug on the way out. "Keep in touch. You have my phone number." Jenny just nodded, tears leaking out the corners of her eyes. Amelia was pretty sure she wouldn't hear from her. There was a connection through shared pain, like prisoners, that didn't really have a reason to persist too long when the trauma was gone. She felt surprisingly light. So her finances would take a hit. France wasn't going anywhere and maybe if she could counter sue, she'd get there even sooner. But no way was she going to count those chickens.

She'd only been slightly bluffing about the attorney. Darnell Williams was a young attorney who sublet space from a temporary staffing agency two floors down. They'd met in the elevator one morning two years ago when Amelia got on before she'd had sufficient sips of her extra grande latte and didn't have her filters up. Not that she had too many of those anyway, but later in the day she never would have said, "You will never get anywhere wearing that tie." Mortified, she'd turned around and faced the elevator doors, but Darnell hadn't let it rest there. He'd followed her out, wanting to know what was wrong with it. As she recalled, it had been a pale lavender with little yellow dots or something. She'd ended up taking him to Nordstrom on her lunch break. He'd told her his caseload doubled as soon as he started wearing her picks and they'd been office buddies ever since. They mostly talked fashion psychology, not just what was hot but what made people respond a certain way. Amelia knew he was out on his own because he'd never quite fit the mold the bigger law firms were looking for. She didn't even know exactly what kind of law he practiced, but she figured he'd be able to recommend someone. She texted him as she got in the elevator.

Amelia: In the office?

Darnell: Always.

Amelia: I just got fired and sued. Do you have space for a new client?

Darnell: What! Get down here.

Amelia: I am here. Agency's not open yet.

She shut off her phone just as Darnell swooped into the darkened lobby and popped open the door.

"Mel, what the heck happened? Last I heard you were off to an island retreat for that gas-turd's wedding." Darnell was the only person in the world allowed to call her Mel, mostly because it made their names rhyme and as he said, they didn't have much else in common.

"Tony got himself murdered."

"Remind me never to go on vacation with you."

Amelia rolled her eyes. There had never been anything romantic between them. Darnell was at least seven years younger, not that would have stopped her for the right guy, but in a lot of ways, they were just too much alike.

"What kind of lawyer are you anyway?"

"The fabulous kind." He tightened the knot on his boldly striped tie.

"What kind of law?" she repeated dryly.

"Oh, property law mostly, but I do some of the smaller stuff too when it's the same client, like wills and estates, that kind of thing."

"Oh good, so can I hire you for some of this? I'm haven't looked at the summons, so I'm not sure what they're accusing me of, but it's tied to property."

"You can be my client, but I'm not going to charge you."

"Darnell, you can't do that. You have bills to pay too."

"And you need to get your ass to France."

She blinked hard. It was nice to have friends. "Well, let's work something out when you understand what's going on. There's bound to be some money from a sale or counter suit or something."

He nodded confused. "You selling your condo?"

"Not yet, but that's an option. Look, Tony was a crook."

"So not news…"

"I mean a real crook. He was using cocaine and blackmailing drug dealers. That island I went to? He owned almost all of it, inherited it when his father died. But he got spooked by his ex-wife and transferred it all to me without my knowing."

"Mel, how do you get yourself into these messes?"

"Maybe I'm cursed. Could you ask your grandma for me?" Darnell glared at her. One night when they'd gone out for drinks after work, he'd let drop that his Jamaican grandmother was a little too into voodoo for his comfort. "I'm serious. Do you know anyone else that can end up being sued for being given an island without their knowledge?"

They'd arrived in the back corner to the small office Darnell rented from the staffing agency. It was quiet and had a window with a glorious mountain view. Amelia was always a little surprised that he got any work done in it. He took his seat behind the glass desk and she plopped into the nearest guest chair, putting her bag on the other.

"Mel. Chicken bones aren't going to get you out of this mess and you don't have any real enemies, so I doubt they got you into it either. Why are you being sued again?"

"Tony transferred the property to me. The police say he was planning to take it back, but he got killed. He also got killed before he married Heather. So now she and her daddy are pissed."

"Ah." He still looked confused, so she handed over the manila envelope. Darnell slit the flap expertly and extracted the paperwork. He read through it, leaning back in his chair and flipping the pages back with a thoughtful expression. "They're suing you for emotional pain and suffering for allowing Tony to be murdered on your property. Basically, for not having sufficient security, etc."

"Oh god." She put her head down on her knees and mumbled through her hair, "how do I defend myself against that?"

"Well you could hire a good defense attorney and I know a few, or…" He paused for dramatic effect. "You get them to drop the case which will be quicker, cheaper and easier."

"Tell me."

"Image management, just like this tie." He smiled as he flipped the end of it up at her. "It's an interesting person that feels this much pain and suffering." He held the manila envelope aloft. "For the loss of someone that was blackmailing an underage girl for sex."

"Okaayy, true. But how?"

"Leave it me." His smile turned wolfish. Amelia was suddenly very glad he was on her side.

"I still think I need to pay you. And I'd really appreciate it if you could look into the property thing and make sure I really do own it. If I do, then I have a lot of decisions to make."

"Tell you what, I'll do all that, but instead of payment you put me up at your…" He flipped the pages of the summons again. "… Ravenswood Inn whenever I like. I could use a getaway pad."

"Deal. As long as I own it, anyway."

They shook hands. "Give me a week and I'll get back to you, okay?"

"Okay. And thanks, Darnell."

"No worries, Mel. You're the secret behind my success."

She rolled her eyes at his hyperbole and let herself out of the office, feeling far better than when she'd arrived. The temp agency had opened and she waved at a few of the bouncy young women rushing around. They were used to seeing her. She went downstairs and hopped on the next bus home.

Chapter 20

❧

Amelia stood in the middle of her small living room and turned a full three hundred and sixty degrees, taking in her surroundings. The place was boring. How had she not seen it before? And it was empty. The tiny little voice inside her added and lonely. Part of her survey was considering whether she was ready to sell up. She wasn't going to do anything rash, at least not until Darnell called, but it didn't hurt to take an inventory and consider her options.

The housing market in Seattle was hot. This was a prime location. Her decor was boring, but well within the much-hyped 'neutral'. She was out of a job so she had nothing keeping her here. It remained to be seen if France was her next destination.

She sighed and plopped down on the love seat, swinging her black legging-covered legs up beside her. A maroon homespun sack dress gave her and the room a little bit of color. She was bored. The last week had been so exciting, normal was no longer enough. She looked out the vertical blinds slit to the city below. It was still raining. The lunch rush was on, with people in black nylon jackets who refused to use an umbrella scurrying down the sidewalk and almost getting killed by the cars coming out of subterranean parking garages. The people who were carrying umbrellas kept them so low they couldn't see where they were going and were playing the same game with death, just at a slower speed. It tickled something in Amelia's funny bone.

She got up and did a little tidying. It didn't help much. She wondered what Gus was up to in his fairy tale cottage in the woods. Maybe he'd only been there to keep an eye on the drug runners and had already left the island. That reminded her and she went over to the tiny hall closet just inside the front door and fetched her pink tote bag. She hadn't really unpacked anything besides her dirty clothes when she arrived home. Now, she pulled out the two books she'd bought on the island, the history and the one on hobbies for busy women. She put them on the small coffee table and went into the kitchen to make some tea. When it was ready, she pulled out a vodka bottle from the cupboard beneath the sink and added a splash. Why not? She wasn't working and didn't have anywhere to be. She took it back into the living room and settled in.

Pulling the history book over first, she leafed through the table of contents until she found the reference to the Three Bears' Cottage on page 198. She flipped through. There was a small and not very good black and white image of the adorable place. But the description was riveting. The building-collecting Mr. Evans had it built after a visit to San Simeon in California and before he went to Europe. Not long after it was built, he gifted it to his children's governess amid rumors of their long-term affair. Considering the proximity of the cottage to the fancy house, Amelia was leaning towards those rumors. She flipped through the book, looking for a color portrait of Mr. Evans. Yep, he'd been blond. That was putting a new spin on Goldilocks.

She set the history book aside with her immediate curiosity satisfied. She really should read the book in the event that she owned most of the island. She should understand what she had, but it could wait. Taking several sips of her fortified tea, she let the warmth settle in her stomach. She clearly needed a hobby, so maybe she should put some effort into that while she waited to see what her future held.

She fell asleep trying to decide if she could be trusted with a quilting needle.

On Wednesday, Darnell called. Unfortunately, he did it while she was at the dentist finally getting some fillings replaced that had been due for over a year. It had occurred to her the day before that her insurance was about to run out and luckily they'd had an opening. Well, if you could count lying there with your mouth open getting drilled for two hours as lucky. It beat the alternative though, she supposed. In any event, she was in no position to answer her phone and when she tried to call him back it went straight to voice mail.

Finally, the next morning she got a hold of him but only because she called at 7:30 on the dot. Darnell was a total creature of habit given the opportunity and always arrived in the office then. Since not many other people knew that, they started calling a lot later.

"Mel! I think we've cracked it."

"Really?"

"Unless you were really hoping to keep that job?"

"Well, I'm still pissed, but I was going to quit soon anyway."

"That's what I thought. So, here's the deal. I was right that Mr. Hammond doesn't want to be associated with drug dealers. Seems little Miss Heather left that part of the story out. But he needs to save a little face 'cause he's already told all his sauna buddies at the club not to hire you."

"Are you kidding me? What a …"

"We both know that, but this is how deals work. Listen up."

She sighed but listened. "So, he's willing to drop the lawsuit if you drop any pursuit of an employment claim and he'll cover your health insurance for a year. You'll get the vested portion of your pension."

Well damn, she could have put that dentist appointment off a little longer. Darnell continued. "You could go after him in court if you want, but it's a gamble. This is a lot safer and you never have to deal with him again."

"Yeah, I'm okay with that. I guess."

"You know there are papers to sign. Can you swing by on Friday at two? I should have everything ready by then."

"Sure, did you get a chance to look into the property at all? That may factor in to what I do next."

"Yeah, I did that first because if you didn't own the hotel, then you'd be free and clear of their silly lawsuit. But you do own it. And everything else listed."

"For sure? He doesn't have a long-lost child that's going to show up and claim it?"

"Wouldn't matter, it was a pre-death gift, not an inheritance. So yeah, it's weird but legal and all yours."

"Right. Well thanks, Darnell. I'll see you on Friday."

Amelia hung up and took a swift breath through her nose. She was unemployed and wealthy. At least in terms of property. Wasn't it weird that she didn't even have keys to any of the places? Who could fix that? Or should she just sell everything outright? She thought about the island now missing twenty-odd residents as they awaited trials on the mainland. No, she couldn't do that to the rest of the islanders. Not yet. She scrolled through her contact list and clicked.

"Ravenswood Inn, how can I help you?"

"Becky? It's Amelia. I'm coming back."

Thank you for reading!

If you enjoyed this story, please leave a review on Amazon. It doesn't have to be long! Follow my author account there to be notified when the next book in the series is available or join my newsletter (see below).

❧

Beth McElla writes cozy mysteries under the majestic evergreens of the Pacific Northwest.

You can find her on Facebook: https://www.facebook.com/Beth-McElla-111419010328702/
Or the website of her alterego: https://www.julietchase.com/beth-mcella

Printed in Great Britain
by Amazon

42092530R00092